I MARRIED WONJIN

A Prime Mating Agency

REGINE ABEL

CONTENTS

I MARRIED WONJIN

She once feared him but now cannot resist him…

After decades of violence, the war pitting the human colony on Cibbos against the Yurus tribe has finally ended. Lara never expected that peace between their species would lead to a romantic entanglement with one of their former enemies. Resembling a cross between an orc and a minotaur, Wonjin looks nothing like how Lara had imagined a potential mate. And yet, she cannot deny the attraction she feels.

When he finally makes his move, how can she refuse this grumpy, cuddly pile of muscles, with the fluffiest fur and cutest ears?

DEDICATION

To those who believe that love is the reunion of two souls meant for each other, regardless of race, culture, gender, religion, appearance, and whatever other barriers society wants to impose on its people. Love freely, love wholly, and seize every moment. Life is too short to waste it trying to please others instead of embracing who we are.

CHAPTER 1
WONJIN

The Zelconian circled around Rihanna's speeder with undisguised fascination. It felt odd standing in such proximity to one of the birds in a peaceful fashion. Despite the truce between the humans, the Zelconians, and my people, the Yurus, we didn't mingle much. After all, the birds rarely came down from their mountain dwellings.

Councilor Dakas was the exception since he had married the human doctor Luana, who continued working in the colony. He shifted his midnight blue wings as he crouched in front of the speeder. His oversized eyes—devoid of pupils or irises but filled with a sea of stars—examined the vehicle. The gold and dark-blue feathers of his crest cast a shadow over his face, making it harder to read his thoughts while Rihanna showed him the speeder.

Her energy and enthusiasm never ceased to amaze me. When Great Chieftain Zatruk had first brought her to Mutarak as his mate, I had laughed at what I believed to be a joke. We'd all known he'd agreed to marry a human through the Prime Mating Agency. Never in a thousand years had any of us imagined it would be with such a tiny little woman. Zatruk was a beast of a male, the most powerful and fearsome among us. Compared to him, Rihanna barely looked more than a child.

But I'd learned at my own expense not to be fooled by her petite stature and fragile appearance. Rihanna's mind was as sharp as her tongue, and she was a cunningly accomplished fighter: the perfect mate for our leader. And she had chosen *me* to protect her while visiting the human colony—a great honor. I took that role seriously, keeping an eye on the humans lurking around to spy on us, while also paying attention to what Rihanna was saying about the speeder. I craved finding out more about this off-worlder technology.

I tensed when a human female quickly approached, ready to protect my clan mistress. But my brain ceased to function after a single look at the woman. In her mid to late twenties, slender, and measuring about 5'8, she was breathtaking. Shoulder-length dark-brown hair, almost the same color as her gorgeous, elongated eyes, a nice pair of pouty lips, and a pointy chin, everything about her called to me. From what I'd read of humans, she would be deemed East Asian, whereas Rihanna was African. But to my mind, she was simply mine.

"Hi," she said, coming to a stop near us. "My name is Lara."

Lara…

Her slightly throaty voice rolled over my skin like a warm summer breeze. I wanted to say her name out loud, over and over again, taste it on my tongue, feel it on my lips. She was the human engineer supposed to come help us.

"It's a pleasure to meet you," Rihanna said with a grin. "This is my friend, Wonjin."

My skin heated, my patches of fur standing on end while my stomach knotted when her dark gaze settled on me. I stood transfixed, my lips parting to utter a greeting, but not a single word came out. Panic swelled within me as I gaped at her like an idiot. To add to my mortification, my wretched ears started flapping like the wings of a bird washing in a pond. The blasted things always did that whenever I felt embarrassed. It was a common trait with Yurus, but mine would just go on flapping endlessly.

"Hi," Lara responded.

She barely spared me a glance, immediately dismissing me to focus her attention on the speeder.

That cut me deeply.

But why would I expect otherwise? By human standards, we were rabid creatures, barely civilized. My peers would describe me as reasonably handsome. To her, I undoubtedly resembled the mythical beast of ancient human lore called a Minotaur—not exactly their definition of beauty.

Still too frozen to respond, even with a mere grunt, I stared at Lara, who almost shoved Dakas out of the way so that she could get a closer look. He chuckled, stepping aside in a playfully apologetic fashion.

Eyes glued on Lara, I swallowed hard at the illogical jealousy that swept through me when she ran a hand over the nose of the speeder in an almost reverent caress. Just as I was berating myself for yet another absurd reaction, the strong impression of being observed had me jerking my head to the right.

My heart dropped, shame and anger surging through me at finding Dakas examining my features. Our gazes locked, and I audibly closed my still gaping mouth, humiliation burning in my gut. The Zelconian tilted his head to the side in a way eerily similar to how birds often did as he studied my reaction. Members of his species were powerful empaths. He had perceived absolutely everything about how Lara's presence was affecting me.

My brown skin darkened, and my thrice cursed ears started flicking again. I could have died with embarrassment to be thus exposed, caught drooling over a human. I averted my eyes, wishing I could turn on my stealth shield and disappear.

"What seems to be the problem?" Lara asked.

"There's no problem with this one," Rihanna replied. "We're

building a few like these and are having performance issues with the engine. We were hoping a new pair of eyes would help our engineers sort it out. Our new ones fly the same as mine, but they can't achieve the same speed and responsiveness."

"Can you show us how this one performs?" Dakas asked.

"Sure!"

Despite my annoyance with myself, I watched with a great deal of admiration—and pride—as our Clan Mistress straddled her hover bike and flew it around the empty plaza of the human colony, right in front of the medical clinic where we'd just visited Luana—Dakas's mate. Even with the limited space, Rihanna achieved some phenomenal speeds, especially once she flew the speeder close to its maximum height of twelve meters. By the time she landed, Lara was beside herself with excitement.

"This is so amazing!" she whispered, staring at the speeder as if it was the greatest wonder in the universe.

Once again, I silently berated myself for feeling annoyed that this pile of metal would stir such awe in Lara while my presence left her completely indifferent.

"It is quite impressive," Dakas concurred. "Could you have gone higher than where you flew?"

Rihanna shook her head. "No, speeders aren't really meant to fly this high. They're designed to hover. Ten to twelve meters above ground is the maximum. But you don't want to remain at such heights for too long. It can get dangerous."

I mostly tuned out the rest of their conversation, too busy staring at Lara while she continued pawing at the speeder. How would such small and delicate hands feel on my fur? On my skin? How soft would her hair be if I ran my fingers through it?

Lara suddenly looking up at Rihanna startled me.

"If it's okay, I'll tag along, too," Lara said with enthusiasm. "I'd like to take a gander at those other speeders and see if I can help, although I make no promises."

Baffled, it took me a second to realize both Dakas and Lara

would be accompanying us back to Mutarak. I inwardly cursed myself for not paying attention to their conversation, as a protector should have.

"Wonderful! You can ride on my speeder with me if you like," Rihanna offered.

Lara squealed with excitement.

As much as I rejoiced that she would stay with us a little longer, I couldn't help feeling a great deal of chagrin watching her settling behind Rihanna on her speeder. She wrapped her slender arms around my Clan Mistress' waist. I wished it was me she was holding like that. Heaving a sigh, I hopped onto the back of my krogi named Cilo. We said our goodbyes to Luana then headed back to Mutarak. Dakas flew overhead, Lara and Rihanna led the way on her speeder, and I rode my beast behind them.

Barely fifteen minutes later, we reached the village. Rihanna having warned him of our incoming visitors, Great Chieftain Zatruk was already waiting for us in the town square. Slightly bigger than me, with his pristine white fur, bright-red eyes, and massive white horns with black tips, our clan leader looked as formidable as he was deadly. In sharp contrast to his raw power, my mother Jerdea stood by his side. Tall and slim, she was the embodiment of Yurus grace and femininity. And right now, she was buzzing with excitement. As our clan's Head Scientist, being able at last to converse with other engineers from more technologically advanced species was a dream come true.

As we closed the distance to them, I pushed my krogi so I would arrive first. I jumped off mid stride and rushed to Rihanna even as she was coming to a stop. Although she clearly didn't need my assistance, I extended a hand to Lara to help her down from the speeder. I had acted on instinct, but now I feared the public humiliation of her potential rejection. She seemed shocked by this unexpected gesture. To my relief, she accepted my hand, placing hers in mine.

Ancestors!

It was so soft, so warm… The oddest mix of possessiveness and protectiveness surged through me. But before I could properly savor her touch, Lara let go of my hand as soon as she was back on her feet and turned to face Zatruk. Despite my disappointment, I took solace in that she didn't see my stupid ears making a spectacle of themselves again.

Dakas landed a couple of meters in front of Zatruk, just as Rihanna was walking up to her mate. Seeing our fearsome Great Chieftain soften as he gently caressed his wife's cheek stirred a powerful longing within me. My eyes flicked towards Lara, my fertile imagination picturing a similar situation between us.

"Zatruk, Jerdea, please meet Lara, one of the engineers of Kastan. She agreed to come have a look at our speeders to see if she could help with the performance issues," Rihanna said. "Lara, this is my husband Zatruk and our Head Scientist, Jerdea."

"It's a delight to have you here," my mother said in a bubbly voice before turning to Dakas. "And you as well, Counci… Dakas."

I barely repressed the urge to roll my eyes. Our females found the Zelconians quite attractive, even though they'd only seen them from a distance. It was the first time one of them had actually set foot inside Mutarak. Unlike the pureblood Zelconians, Dakas had inherited a great deal of his human father's features like a mouth and nose instead of a beak, and feet and legs in lieu of bird feet with talons. I could see why they would find him attractive, despite his bluish skin and golden down feathers on his broad chest.

"We are both eager to see what you have accomplished," Dakas replied.

"Yeah, definitely," Lara echoed. "Thank you for welcoming us," she added, looking at Zatruk, appearing somewhat intimidated.

Another irrational bout of jealousy and envy flared deep within me at the way she acknowledged Zatruk when she'd barely paid me any attention. But then, I was just a grunt, the village idiot according to many.

"Do not mention it," Zatruk said politely. "If you would follow me, the development facility is right here."

I almost followed them before remembering I still needed to take care of my mount.

"I will go park your speeder while I stable Cilo," I offered.

"Thank you. You're very kind," Rihanna said with genuine gratitude.

Rihanna said krogis looked like a dragon and a bull had a baby. While I could see the resemblance to a bull in its general shape and face, the smattering of scales on the beast didn't seem sufficient to justify the link with a dragon. Thankfully, it didn't frighten her, nor did it seem to scare Lara. As much as I admired the speeders we were working on, I preferred riding a krogi any day. That they were formidable battle partners increased their appeal.

I couldn't help but smile as I watched Rihanna leave hand-in-hand with Zatruk, my mother and our guests following them to the research center located on the other side of the town square. She and I had a rough start, in large part due to my own stupidity. Since, she had earned my undying loyalty not only with her kindness and dedication helping to save my people, but also by getting the human doctor Luana to cure me of the disability that had plagued my entire existence.

After stabling my beast and dropping Rihanna's speeder inside Zatruk's forge, I hurried back to the research center. It was one of the most imposing buildings in the village. Multiple workstations lined the walls of the large, open space. Most of them faced the immense windows looking out on the square. Some of the speeders we'd been working on stood next to a workstation, hooked with cables to the computer running tests and diagnostics on them.

I approached just as Zatruk was finishing making the introductions. Once again, I repressed the urge to roll my eyes at our female engineers fawning all over Dakas. A part of me wanted to feel offended that our best and brightest should be getting so hot over a bird. But then, Yurus males didn't exactly impress with their wits. It wasn't that they weren't intelligent. Many of my clanmates actually possessed the capacity to be brilliant. But Blood Rage consumed their lives. The need for constant battle prevented them from investing in more intellectual pursuits.

Glancing back at Dakas, I could see how the gentle and sweet way he interacted with our females further endeared him to them. However, the shy, almost embarrassed way in which he responded to so much fawning attention took me aback. Zelconians always seemed so cold, in control, borderline emotionless that I hadn't expected such a behavior from him.

My mother beginning to show the speeders to our guests reclaimed my attention.

"These are the three we've built so far," Mother said, pointing at the two bikes in the center of the space, and then at the third one sitting on the testing device next to the main workstation.

My heart leapt in my chest as Lara headed straight for the blue speeder. Her eyes sparked with awe as she slowly circled around it, her fingertips brushing over the sleek curves of the chassis.

"These are absolutely stunning," she said in a wistful voice. "Especially this one. It's my favorite."

An overwhelming wave of pride surged through me.

"Thank you," I said, having found my voice again in her presence.

Lara's head jerked up, and she turned to look at me, wide-eyed. "You made this?"

I shifted on my hooves, unable to decide if I felt more flattered by her awe than offended by her shock that this could be my work.

"I smithed the chassis and frame," I said, my stupid grumpy voice coming back with a vengeance.

"Smithed? As in you did this by hand?" she asked, looking flabbergasted.

"Yes," I said, my tone making it clear it should be obvious. "Deutenium isn't meant for machines. You have to listen to the metal and make it sing to bend it to your will."

"Wow, you're really talented," Lara said, sounding impressed.

My skin warmed at the compliment and genuine admiration emanating from her. Ancestors, if this is how it felt to be seen by her, I never wanted Lara to take her eyes off me.

"My son is also very good with math and physics," Mother interjected proudly. "Wonjin does most of the calculations for our buildings, just for fun."

Lara's jaw dropped at the same time as Rihanna's. Zatruk's and Dakas' brows shot up. That the others hadn't known didn't surprise me, but I had thought our Great Chieftain would have known of my scientific skills, or at least suspected them. But then, as younglings, while I'd been busy studying, he'd been busy fighting. Nurturing my mind with knowledge opened the doors to countless possibilities otherwise denied to me by my prior injury.

"It's just a hobby," I mumbled, feeling self-conscious as Lara continued to look at me as if she was finally seeing me for the first time. "But once we've sorted the performance problems of the speeder, I can make one for you, if you wish."

My own words took me by surprise. I hadn't planned on making such an offer. But now that I had, I silently congratulated myself for blurting out such an insightful idea. Lara clearly loved the speeders. Beyond my desire to please her, it would give me an excuse to talk with her and get her to know me.

"What?! Oh no! I can't accept that," Lara exclaimed, stunned.

I stiffened and frowned in confusion. "You do not wish to own one?"

Lara hesitated, her lovely face taking on an uncomfortable expression.

"Well… uhm… actually, yes. Who wouldn't? But I can't accept such an expensive gift."

I blinked, my confusion going up a notch. "It is not expensive. It is only my time and skills," I replied, wondering where this notion of cost had come from.

"Consider it compensation for helping us fix the performance issues," Rihanna interjected.

Lara opened and closed her mouth a few times before casting a helpless look at Dakas. Another wave of jealousy reared its head, and I barely repressed a menacing growl at the Zelconian Councilor. He didn't deserve such a sign of aggression on my part, but I hated that my woman sought his advice in response to a present I wanted to give her. But Dakas simply smiled, seeming amused by the situation. I shifted on my hooves, a sense of annoyance crawling up my spine that he knew exactly what I was feeling. With his eyes filled with stars, without pupils or irises, I couldn't say for sure whether he was looking at me. But my gut said he was. The corner of his lips quirking up ever so slightly seemed to confirm it.

"I guess if I manage to help you guys, it would indeed be a fair trade," Lara conceded at last in an uncertain voice.

"Then I will make you one. It is settled," I said in a tone that brooked no argument, genuinely baffled by her reluctance.

"Okay, then," Lara said, looking both thrilled and slightly overwhelmed.

Ancestors, if she was going to respond in such an irrational fashion when given an opportunity to indulge in things she wanted, wooing her was going to prove quite challenging. That didn't scare me. Nothing of value was ever easily won.

Looking extremely pleased, my mother proceeded to explain to both Dakas and Lara what the problems were. A part of me wished she would have let me cover those technical aspects so that I could show off my knowledge to Lara. But she had no reason to suspect my sudden infatuation and, as our Head Scientist, it was my mother's role to present our project.

Despite that, I still got an opportunity to shine as the discussion shifted from engine and programming issues to technical questions regarding the metal we used to build the speeders, the assembly process, the way the engine interacted with the chassis, our heating and cooling systems, as well as a variety of other technical factors. I was in my element, firing quick and precise answers to everything they threw our way.

As much as I wanted to monopolize the discussion to impress Lara, I reined myself in, and allowed Zatruk to also display his knowledge as a master smith. Although he hadn't planned for this, my Great Chieftain had realized what a blessed gift his mate had given us by luring a human engineer and a Zelconian Councilor to our village. Our entire future depended on our ability to build high-performing speeders. By displaying how smart and competent we actually were, instead of the brutish idiots they believed us to be, we could secure a much-needed alliance.

By the glimmer of respect in Dakas's eyes, and the way Lara clung to our every word, we had successfully impressed them beyond expectations.

"From what I can see, you do not have a construction problem, but a programming one," Dakas said at last, pointing at the monitor of the computer hooked to the speeder. "You have three systems sending conflicting commands to run their respective subroutines. In isolation, each system works perfectly, but see, this command to prevent overheating essentially also caps the engine's ability to reach higher speeds, as it's imposing the same heat restrictions."

"*Jaafan!*" my mother whispered, her words echoing my thoughts. She leaned in, her eyes flicking between the two strings of code. "How did we not see this before?"

How, indeed? I felt like a monumental idiot. How had I not realized this after going over every single line of this code, over and over again?

"Because it's not obvious," Dakas said in a gentle tone. "I only figured it out this quickly because I spent three months banging my head on the walls trying to fix a similar problem with one of our underground transport systems in Synsara before I finally realized what was happening."

"Ugh, then we are blessed that the Goddess sent you our way. We cannot afford to waste three months on solving such a problem. Time is of the essence," my mother said.

Dakas tilted his head to the side. "Why is that? What do you intend to do with these speeders?"

Mother glanced at Zatruk. Following her gaze, Dakas turned to our clan leader to study his features... probably his emotions as well.

"Would you mind telling me about your plans?" Dakas asked.

I held my breath. This could be a turning point for us. With the help of the humans and Zelconians, our chances of success and of saving our people would significantly increase. But what if they decided instead to sabotage our efforts? Despite the truce between our peoples, humans had little love for us. After all, we had bullied them for years. The Zelconians didn't need us. They were the most technologically advanced species among the three. In a head-to-head war, they would obliterate us.

Zatruk eyed him silently for a brief moment before giving him a sharp nod. "Yes, but not here."

"Do you mind continuing without me for now?" Dakas asked Lara.

"No, we're good!" Lara said with enthusiasm. "We're probably going to have to do a lot of rewriting to work around these conflicts. We should be quite busy."

"Very well," Dakas said.

Zatruk gestured for the Zelconian to follow. He caressed Rihanna's cheek then left with Dakas. I shifted my focus back to the woman I intended to claim as mine.

CHAPTER 2
LARA

The past three weeks working with the Yurus on the speeders still felt surreal. Even before my birth, every human in Kastan lived in fear of our belligerent neighbors. They would regularly raid our village, steal our harvest, randomly destroy stuff, and rough up the few fools who dared stand in their way. To me, they had always been nothing but brutish savages. To be sitting in their midst, working side-by-side, and sharing their meals still broke my brain.

They were nothing like what I had imagined and been raised to believe.

I'd expected to be tiptoeing around a city littered with bloodied, unconscious bodies from all the brawling, females cowering in fear from the brutish males that kept them in constant terror, and to see everyone systematically looking over their shoulders to avoid getting stabbed in the back. Instead, I'd found a clean, well-maintained city, surprisingly advanced despite its limited access to the galactic network, and a total absence of crime.

Granted, their males fought a lot, but it was nothing like the bloodthirsty rampages I'd envisioned. They kept their brawling to the town square, with the crowd cheering them on, while the females usually looked on with an unimpressed expression.

The females weren't terrified victims. They were truly the backbone of this society. Considering how violent the males were when fighting each other, the gentle, caring way in which they handled their females truly boggled my mind. Was I not seeing it with my own eyes, I never would have believed it.

Even the brawling wasn't the gory mayhem our folktales had claimed them to be. Yes, they went all out on each other. But the minute one of the fighters looked injured or lost consciousness, someone pulled them out of the fight. No one pounded on an opponent clearly defeated or unable to defend himself.

More importantly, the fights were extremely few and far between, not the constant pummeling I'd been led to believe took place here. Then again, all the males were busy smithing, either making new chassis for the speeders or building weapons for sale to the intergalactic community.

My gaze roamed over the wide-open space of the research center where a dozen Yurus females continued to work on improving the performance of the bikes. They would indeed make formidable prizes for their battle arena project, especially if the Yurus convinced the Zelconians to get on board and allow them to use their crystals as a power source. It would make these speeders the best ones in the galaxy.

Beyond my nerdy desire to see it happen for the bragging rights of having partaken in such an amazing project, I wanted this to work for greater reasons. The success of the battle arena of the Yurus meant prolonged peace between our two colonies. With the Yurus finally having a permanent venue to exert their biological need for violence, we would no longer serve as their punching bags. It also meant significant opportunities for prosperity and access to galactic resources and technologies for all three species on this planet.

All of us, third generation colonists, were dying for greater access to all of this. Our ancestors had left Earth specifically to start anew with a simple life and more traditional values, devoid of the trappings of technology. The younger people like me, born into this, chafed at all those restrictions. Beyond the fact that we felt like we were stagnating, this mentality had also kept us in a vulnerable position against the Yurus as we had lacked the technology to defend ourselves against more powerful enemies.

So this project meant a lot to us as well.

But to get the Zelconians *and* convince the leader of our human colony to join in on this project, we needed to get these speeders in tip top shape. They were already pretty amazing, but pushing the speed limit just a wee bit higher would make them perfect. Unfortunately, while the engine could withstand it, we kept running into stability issues that we couldn't quite sort out.

Just as those thoughts were crossing my mind, the large garage doors of the research center parted. Seeing the massive silhouette of Wonjin walking in once again stirred the oddest mix of emotions in me. I didn't know what to make of him. He always looked disgruntled—as seemed to be the case with every male of his species. And yet, he systematically went out of his way to provide everything and anything the females needed, myself included.

More importantly, although he didn't speak much, on the rare occasions he did it was usually incredibly smart. That, too, messed with my mind.

To my surprise, he headed straight for me, carrying a large temperature-controlled container. I shifted uneasily in my seat as he closed the distance between us. His dark eyes leveled at me held the most unnerving intensity. Then again, he always had this intense way of staring at me. Before the truce between our people, it would have sent me running for the hills. He looked like he wanted to bash my head in to see what lay inside.

"Hello, Lara," Wonjin said in his usual grumpy tone, as if it pained him to have to make conversation.

"Hello, Wonjin," I said cautiously.

"Did the modifications work?" he asked.

I blinked, unsure as to what he was referring to. "Modifications?"

"Mother said you were having issues with increasing the speed," he said with a frown as if I should have known exactly what he was referring to.

"Yes," I replied, still uncertain what this was about. "I'm still working on solving the issue."

"I modified one of the speeders so that it should fit with your specs. I made the fuselage narrower and readjusted the weight distribution so that it would remain stable even at greater speeds. Did my mother not tell you?" he asked, pointing at one of the two speeders behind my workstation.

My stomach dropped as I stared at it before looking back at Wonjin with a mortified expression. Jerdea had indeed mentioned that her son had brought me a new speeder more than three days ago.

"Oh, my God! I'm so sorry!" I exclaimed, pressing a hand to my burning cheeks. "She did mention it to me, but I thought it was just a new chassis. I didn't realize you had modified it to help address some of my issues. Therefore, I didn't touch it because I wanted to fix the problem first before setting up another speeder."

Wonjin just stood there, staring at me with a completely unreadable expression. His sole response to my apology was a single grunt. I would have preferred him soundly berating me than this stoic reaction. Although he looked unbothered, at a visceral level my gut told me my perceived indifference or dismissal of his work had deeply hurt him.

"I'll test it right away," I offered, feeling like a total shit.

"You don't have to, if you found a different way to approach your issue," he grumbled.

"No! I absolutely have not. I'm just as stumped as I've been for the past few days," I said, jumping to my feet and hurrying to unhook the speeder currently connected to the analysis computers.

Wonjin grunted again. Putting down his container next to my workstation, he moved the speeder as soon as I finished unhooking it before swiftly bringing me the one he had modified. To my dismay, he remained disturbingly close to me as I started hooking this one to my computer. That male was freaking massive. His biceps alone were bigger than my head. Next to him, I always felt incredibly fragile and vulnerable.

Forcing myself to act enthusiastic to hide my nervousness, I gave him a big smile and launched a simulation on the speeder. It started smoothly with a discreet hum, the sound pitching as the speed steadily increased. Wonjin's stare weighed heavily on me, making me squirm. I kept my eyes glued to the monitor, fighting the urge to glance in his direction. My stupid mind kept picturing him with glowing red eyes, shark teeth bared, and massive hands fisted as he itched to smack the living daylights out of me for snubbing his work this long.

It was an irrational reaction on my part as he'd never once raised his voice to me or any of the other females. But for a reason I could never explain, Wonjin always made me feel on edge, like he was going to do or say something that would turn my world upside down forever.

So much for me taking pride in my scientific and rational thinking.

But all such silly thoughts flew right out of my mind when the line on the graph remained steady even as we approached the critical point... then passed it. My jaw dropped. I jerked my head left to glance at the speeder, then right to look back at the monitor.

All systems were green, the line on the graph remained steady, and no warnings had gone off.

Slowly turning my head, I stared in disbelief at Wonjin over my shoulder. Lifting his chin, he crossed his muscular arms over his massive chest and made a sniffing sound with a smuggest expression plastered all over his face. Under different circumstances, I might have laughed. But I was way too stunned.

I glanced back at the monitor, which continued to show the test was successful.

"Fuck me sideways," I whispered in disbelief.

"Excuse me?!" Wonjin exclaimed.

I stiffened, my cheeks all but bursting into flames when I realized what I'd just said.

"It's… uh… Never mind that. It's just a silly human expression to indicate shock," I mumbled.

Once again, Wonjin merely grunted and went back to staring at me. Fuck my life. I'd give anything to know what thoughts were bubbling in that big head of his.

"But wow, you truly fixed it," I said, eager to shift the subject and attention away from me. "How?"

"I looked at your calculations. Total mass and wind resistance needed to be rectified. So I fixed it," Wonjin said matter-of-factly. "I will send you the specifications on the modifications I made. Once you have done all the other tests you require and are confident it meets your needs, I will adjust the other speeders."

"That's… Wow… Thank you," I said, still blown away.

I'd been banging my head on this damn thing for a week. He'd solved it in half that time. In his shoes, I'd be strutting my stuff, bragging about my awesomeness. He was just like *'Yeah, fixed it. Next?'*

To my surprise, Wonjin tilted his head to the side, giving me a funny look. "Why are you thanking me? *You* are helping *us* solve our problems. It is *I* who thanks *you*."

I opened and closed my mouth, words failing me. What the heck was I supposed to answer? Technically, he was right. Good heavens, why did I always feel so brain-dead and pathetic every time I interacted with that male? He probably thought I was a bumbling idiot.

When the silence stretched, becoming increasingly uncomfortable, Wonjin grunted again, like one would when giving up on a hopeless case. I felt mortified. I usually had a sharp tongue and quick wits. You'd never think so watching me now.

"I brought this back for you from my hunt," Wonjin grumbled, pointing at the temperature-controlled container.

"Oh?" I said, my brow shooting up in surprise.

I stopped the simulation and went to crouch by the container. What could he have possibly brought me that needed to be preserved like that? Cibbos' wilderness was extremely dangerous in many areas. You didn't venture out there alone. Even the most seasoned Yurus hunters rarely took such a risk. But our world contained countless treasures just waiting to be claimed by those strong and skilled enough to venture beyond the safe paths.

Burning with curiosity, I released the latch from the lid. It made a soft hiss, and cool air wafted to me when I lifted it. My face fell, and my brain froze upon peering at the contents.

"A dead bird?" I blurted out, while staring at Wonjin in disbelief.

He bristled. "It's not just *'a dead bird'* but a Moon Hawk," Wonjin said, clearly offended by my reaction.

Moon Hawk or not, it was still a dead bird. What in the world did he expect me to do with that? Why would he ever think I'd want something like this?

"Okay?" I replied, at a loss as to what my response should be.

"They only dwell in the most dangerous parts of Cibbos and are nearly impossible to capture," Wonjin said, sounding like he was questioning my intelligence. "They are a rare delicacy."

"Oh! I see…" I said, trying to sound enthusiastic, while still freaked by why he would think I wanted that. "That's very thoughtful of you."

By the look on his face, I'd miserably failed at sounding pleased by his gift. Although it flitted through his dark brown eyes so fast I almost missed it, the glimmer of his disappointment cut me deep. I knew what it was like to go out of your way to do something nice for someone only to have them casually dismiss it.

He grunted before looking back at my monitor. "I will let you get back to your tasks. Let me know when you've concluded your tests so that I can adjust the other speeders."

"Okay, will do. And thanks again for… everything," I said clumsily, waving in turn at the speeder and at the cooler.

With one final grunt, Wonjin turned around and walked away. I squeezed my eyes shut, and heaved a sigh, my shoulders slouching as I felt like a total shit. He'd just tried to be nice, and I made my best display of how socially challenged I could be. The sound of his hooves resonated loudly as he stomped out, his tail stiff.

I groaned inwardly as some of the females cast furtive glances my way, their gazes lingering on the temperature-controlled container with speculative expressions. Although I doubted they had overheard our conversation, Wonjin's stiff departure would set a few tongues wagging.

Just as he was exiting, Rihanna walked in. She gave him a beaming smile, but he merely nodded at her before continuing on his way out. Rihanna stopped dead in her tracks to watch him walk away with a baffled expression. Once he faded from view, she glanced back inside with a frown, clearly looking for the cause of his odd mood. A single look at my face gave me away. She bit her bottom lip and cast another look towards the now closed door, the oddest sympathetic expression on her face.

What's going on?

She waved at the other females in greeting before making a beeline for me. I liked Rihanna. The petite black woman looked deceivingly delicate in her sleeveless blue maxi dress and matching sandals. Yet, she was all fire and sass. To this day, I didn't understand how she could be so happily married to the Yurus clan leader. Considering the tense relationship between our species, who would have imagined Great Chieftain Zatruk would have been paired with a human?

"Hey, Lara," Rihanna said, as she came to a stop next to my workstation.

"Hey, Rihanna," I replied, bracing for what would follow.

"Is everything okay?" she asked, leaning against the side of my desk.

"Everything is great!" I said with a bit too much enthusiasm. "Wonjin solved our speed problems. He'd actually solved it a few days back, but I'd misunderstood Jerdea's message."

"I'm not surprised," Rihanna said, puffing out her chest like a proud mother, even though they weren't related at all. "People keep underestimating just how brilliant Wonjin is."

Although she said it in a general and nonchalant way, I distinctly felt this was targeted at me.

I shifted on my feet, feeling incredibly self-conscious. "There's no question he's extremely smart. He keeps impressing me. Frankly, helping the Yurus on this project has opened my eyes as to who they really are and their culture. They're nothing like what I imagined."

"Has it?" Rihanna challenged, crossing her arms over her chest.

It was my turn to bristle at that. "Yes, it has," I said firmly. "Working with these females and interacting with other members of the clan has put to rest many of the preconceived notions I had about the Yurus. They're actually pretty cool. I wouldn't still be here after three weeks if I thought otherwise."

Rihanna nodded, still trying to look nonchalant, but I didn't miss the glimmer of approval in her pitch-black eyes.

"Well, we're certainly grateful for your help getting this project off the ground. And I'm especially happy you guys sorted out the speed issues. It will significantly help promote the event," she said in a friendly tone.

"It will. For what it's worth, I really want this to succeed, for both the Yurus and more selfish reasons," I confessed.

"I don't doubt it," Rihanna said softly. "However, I would have expected Wonjin to be more cheerful after contributing to such a victory. Yet, he seemed a little upset. Have you found a different problem?"

The innocent way in which she asked the question didn't fool me in the least. She was fishing. Normally, I would play dumb as I hated people prying into my affairs. But in this instance, I could use some enlightenment from someone who knew the Yurus— and especially Wonjin—much better than I did, and probably ever would.

"No, everything is fine with the speeder. However, I may have bruised his feelings," I added sheepishly.

A worried expression descended over Rihanna's face. "Bruised his feelings, how?"

I cast a guilty glance at the cooler before looking back at her. "He brought me the strangest gift. It really took me by surprise, and my reaction wasn't as enthusiastic as he likely hoped."

"Strange how?" Rihanna insisted, her eyes locking on the container as if she could see through it.

"You know, the kind of weird stuff a cat would bring you," I said, feeling horrible for expressing out loud the thought that had crossed my mind when I first opened the cooler.

Rihanna froze. I couldn't tell if her expression conveyed worry at what I might have said, or concern over what the gift might have been. Without a word, she went and opened the cooler. I held my breath while she peered inside. Her shock gave way to awe, throwing me for a loop. She jerked her head up to look at me like an upset parent would while waiting for their bratty child to explain themselves.

"It's a dead bird!" I said in a tone that made it clear I expected her to side with me.

This time, I felt myself wither at the truly horrified look Rihanna gave me.

"Please tell me you didn't say that to him?" Rihanna pleaded.

I shifted on my feet and twisted my fingers in front of me. "Uh… I may have?"

Rihanna dropped her head and covered her face with both hands while emitting a disbelieving grunt. Although I still didn't know what I'd done wrong—beyond hurting his feelings—I was now fearing I had done some major cultural faux pas or greatly insulted him.

"That bad?" I asked in a small voice.

She dropped her hands and looked at me like I was beyond redemption. Rihanna closed the lid and rose from her crouching position.

"You and I need to talk," Rihanna said in a stern voice before gesturing at my chair. "Have a seat."

For such a small woman, barely 5' to my 5'8, she exuded an incredible aura of strength and authority. I didn't even think twice and complied.

She hoisted herself at the edge of my desk and stared me straight in the eyes. "It's not a 'dead bird' that the cat dragged in, but a Moon Hawk offered to you as a great sign of respect and admiration," Rihanna said sternly. "It is a kingly gift."

"Really?" I asked, feeling even guiltier.

"Really. Moon Hawks are nearly impossible to catch. Experienced hunters lose their lives trying. They are not only extremely hard to reach since they dwell in the most savage regions of Cibbos, but they are also insanely vicious. I am floored that he managed to capture one on his own. No wonder he was gone for three days," Rihanna said, looking like she wanted to smack some sense into me. "This is the kind of present a clan leader would bring to another chieftain to sue him for peace. It's what a male would bring the most sought-after female in the village to ask for her hand in marriage."

My jaw dropped, and my eyes nearly popped out of my head. "What?!"

"Any Yurus female would be fanning herself over such a display of strength and devotion, even if she ended up not choosing him," Rihanna said.

"What the fuck are you saying?" I asked, refusing to accept the obvious.

"That Wonjin is head over heels—well, hooves—for you!" she exclaimed as if it was self-evident. "Didn't you notice how he looks at you as if you were an angel descended from the heavens? How he always tries to please you and provide for anything you need?"

I shook my head, wondering if we were still talking about the same person. "Wonjin glares and grunts! When we're together, the silence is thick enough to cut with a freaking chainsaw! He constantly looks like he wants to bash my head in!"

Rihanna rolled her eyes. "He's not glaring and grunting, he's admiring and purring. If he doesn't speak, it's because your beauty renders him speechless. He doesn't want to bash your head in. He wants to smother you in hugs and cuddles! You do not understand what kind of fluffy teddy bears Yurus males are!"

I stared at her in complete shock, wondering what the hell kind of funky mushroom she'd eaten. Yeah, I could be pretty clueless when it came to realizing a man had the hots for me. But Wonjin?!

"He's a massive Yurus, with horns, tusks, a tail, and hooves. And I'm—"

"A small human with none of those traits," Rihanna interrupted before gesturing at herself. "What's your point?"

I scrunched my face, robbed of any argument. She was smaller than me and married to a much bigger Yurus than Wonjin.

Rihanna's face suddenly softened, and she gave me a sympathetic smile. "Look, I get it. When Kayog told me that the only way to avoid landing on the prison planet Molvi was to marry a giant albino minotaur, I didn't exactly jump for joy. Horns, fur, tusks, tails, and hooves didn't feature high on my checklist for a mate. It's still early in my relationship with him, but Zatruk is freaking awesome. Do not allow preconceptions and societal standards make you miss out on something potentially wonderful. I don't know if you two are a perfect match, but I know Wonjin really has it bad for you. You don't have to rush into anything, or even date him at all if you're not feeling it. But keep an open mind."

Feeling overwhelmed, I tried to make sense of the various thoughts and emotions rushing through me. Without waiting for my response, Rihanna hopped down the edge of my desk and gave my shoulder an encouraging squeeze.

"And eat that bird," she added, pointing at the cooler with her chin. "It is best roasted on a spit."

With that, she strutted away to the workstation at the other end of the room to speak with another one of the engineers.

CHAPTER 3
LARA

Two weeks later, with wind blowing in my hair, I leaned forward on my zeebis to get a better view of Mutarak, the Yurus village below. My mount stopped flapping its wings as it glided down to begin its descent. The native creature, with the body of an Ibex ram, the furry collar of a sheep, and the wingspan of an albatross, constituted the main form of transportation for humans, both on the ground and in the air.

And right now, it was taking me to see the progress Wonjin had made on the speeder he had offered to build for me. No words could express the depth of my excitement.

I still couldn't believe humans and Yurus were collaborating on a massive project. Yet, for all that, some things never changed…

Long before my zeebis landed, I shook my head at another brawl happening in the town square. The Yurus females, standing around the edges with their young and other gawkers, stared with resignation at the two dozen males beating the living daylights out of each other. There was a time when this would have had me running for my life. Now, I knew better.

As soon as I touched down, I dismounted and led my zeebis

to the stables before returning to the square. A few people in the crowd smiled or nodded at me. Despite my height of 5'8, I still felt tiny among them every time I visited. Males and females alike towered over me by a good head.

The Yurus resembled minotaurs with orcish faces, from the forward-facing pair of horns, flappy bull ears and tail, unguligrade legs with hooves, and small tusks framing their mouths. Although delicate patches of fur graced their shoulders, arms, and thighs, they didn't qualify as fur balls. Their various shades of skin and fur color pretty much matched the human spectrum. All of them covered their modesty with a loincloth or a short skirt, which reminded me of the ones ancient Roman gladiators wore. Where the males walked about bare-chested, the females covered their much smaller breasts—compared to a human woman—with a sash in a similar palette to their skirts.

My gaze glided over the writhing mass of muscular bodies brawling. It took seconds for it to lock on to Wonjin's familiar silhouette. Big and brawny, with lustrous hazelnut fur, he was a force to be reckoned with. Quite a few of the other fighters were giving him a wide berth. The not-so-lucky opponent who had taken him on was undoubtedly regretting that decision as Wonjin effortlessly lifted him with one hand before slamming him onto the stone pavement of the square. I winced in sympathetic pain. Wonjin roared in his opponent's face, striking his own chest with both fists, as if daring the male to get back up.

He wisely chose to remain on his back.

Wonjin looked around for the next target when he noticed me. The bloodthirsty fire filling the inky depths of his eyes instantly faded as they widened in surprise. Battle rage bleeding out of him, he made his way towards me only for a beige-furred Yurus to come charging him. My worried gasp turned to one of awe when Wonjin adroitly dodged the attack, backhanding the would-be aggressor so savagely, it sounded like thunderclap. The beige Yurus flew backwards, landing heavily on the ground with a loud thud.

The male shook his head, looking merely slightly stunned by a blow that would have undoubtedly shattered the bones of a human. He swiftly jumped back onto his hooves, seeming ready to charge Wonjin again. But the latter pointed a thick warning finger at him, the almost feral look on his face making it clear he needed to stand down or there would be hell to pay. The beige Yurus hesitated, then wisely heeded the warning, searching for someone else to brawl with.

Wonjin looked terrifying with his menacing expression, massive body, and thick muscles bulging as he bunched them up to appear even more intimidating. A month ago, I'd have peed myself and made my peace with God. Today, did it make me a freak that I found it hot?

He walked up to me with a bit of swagger in his steps. I couldn't say if he was showing off for me. Yurus naturally had an enticingly masculine way of walking. It had been two weeks since Rihanna bluntly pointed out that Wonjin was interested in me. While the thought of being romantically involved with an orc-minotaur had initially horrified me—especially considering the violent history between our people—Rihanna's comment had planted a seed that had taken root. Since then, more than once, I'd caught myself looking for signs that he was indeed interested and asking myself what I'd do about it.

"Lara," he said as a sole greeting as he came to a stop in front of me, his voice vibrating with a deep rumble that I now found quite sexy.

"Wonjin," I said, echoing his greeting. "I see you've been playing with your friends."

He snorted. "I was."

"What started that one? Someone laughed too loudly?" I asked teasingly.

Wonjin grinned, an amused glimmer sparking in his eyes. It

softened his features in the most wondrous fashion. Rihanna's words, that he fell speechless in my presence because he was intimidated, had not fallen on deaf ears. Since, I'd taken to initiating the conversation, and he'd eagerly jump right in. The fearsome Yurus was turning out to be just a really shy nerd.

"Garok flicked his tail. The tip hit Tarmek, who took it as an offense. He shoved him. Garok stumbled back and bumped into Selsan," Wonjin explained.

"Who felt disrespected so shoved him, too. And next thing you know, a third of you guys were bashing each other's heads in for no particular reason," I concluded for him, shaking my head in a way to say they were hopeless cases.

He shrugged with an unrepentant expression. "It's fun."

My gaze roamed over him in an assessing once over. "Well, I'm glad you had fun, but you still got wounded. We need to go clean that up."

Wonjin stiffened, shocked by my comment. He spread his arms and glanced down at himself looking for the wound.

"Up there, silly. Above your right eyebrow. You'd think you would have felt a wound close enough it might have taken your eye out," I said in a reproving tone.

Wonjin's right hand flew to his forehead. His dark eyes widened in shock and then in outrage when his fingers touched the blood from the cut. He jerked his head right to look back at the males still brawling, appearing intent on going to further spank whoever had given him that cut.

"Nuh uh! No more fighting for you today," I warned sternly, grabbing his forearm to bring his attention back to me.

Did it ever.

He stared at my hand on him, the oddest expression flitting over his face before looking back at me. I immediately felt self-conscious. Although we had interacted often over the past few weeks while working on a design for our project, I couldn't recall ever deliberately touching him like this. The small patch of hazelnut fur on his forearm felt incredibly soft and silky, and the muscles beneath surprisingly firm and yet supple. To my dismay, I found myself wondering what it would feel like in his embrace.

Embarrassed, I forced myself to remove my hand casually before continuing to admonish him. "First, we're going to clean that wound. Then you can show me what you needed my feedback on, regarding the speeder."

Wonjin scrunched his face, his thick eyebrows furrowing. "It's just a scratch. Cleansing is—"

"Not open for debate," I interrupted. "You may be big and strong, infection doesn't care."

"I am a Yurus! We—"

"You have a kick ass immune system and accelerated healing once your adrenalin and whatever other hormonal cocktail coursing through your veins kicks into action," I said with an unimpressed tone—even though I was—interrupting him again. "But I'm not letting you take chances. You're too important to this project to let you fall sick over something preventable."

That seemed to knock the wind out of him. Then, right on cue, his cute bull ears started flapping in that telltale sign of Wonjin being embarrassed. While his brown skin, a lighter shade than his hazelnut fur, did a good job of hiding his blushing, his ears systematically gave him away. It was stinking adorable.

I hadn't even meant to flatter him. But Wonjin hadn't been accustomed to praise. Growing up, an injury had made him the favorite target of bullies. And yet, he'd grown into one of the strongest males of his clan and was definitely the smartest. Being the only son of the Head Scientist of his clan didn't hurt. His mother Jerdea was as brilliant as she was delightful.

As was his wont when feeling self-conscious, Wonjin merely grunted in response and gestured for me to follow him. I bit the inside of my cheeks not to grin and fell into step with him, the ruckus of the brawl still rising behind us. There was something endearing about a grumpy male.

To think I used to find him creepy and intimidating.

We didn't go to the research center, which framed the town square to the north, but traveled a few blocks to Wonjin's dwelling. Like every Yurus, he possessed a personal forge at home. His people were masters in the art of molding deutenium, the strongest metal in the galaxy, which was exclusively found on our homeworld. Where every human child learned how to ride a bike, Yurus younglings learned to handle a hammer. And Wonjin definitely qualified as a master.

We entered the forge directly through its external door. I had yet to see inside Wonjin's house. But judging by how neatly he kept his forge, I expected to find the same orderly minimalism in the other rooms—should I ever get to visit them one day.

"Tsk, tsk," I said, giving him another unimpressed look when he made a beeline for the speeder in the right corner of the room, covered with a dark blue tarp. "Bring me the med kit first."

He made another face at me, and yet he complied. I secretly suspected he liked me fussing over him. As he walked out of the forge through the door connecting to the house, I caught myself staring at the round globes of his firm behind that his loincloth barely hid. Although he didn't notice, I averted my eyes, my cheeks burning with embarrassment.

Stepping closer to the forge, I admired the massive set of hammers Wonjin used simultaneously to bend deutenium to his will. Once more, it reminded me of just how insanely strong the Yurus were. Even with both hands, I would struggle to lift a single one of those hammers.

The sound of Wonjin's hoofs heralded his return. As soon as he entered, I gestured at a stool near the workbench on the left. It tickled me pink to see him comply without a word. Back when I used to cower in terror as the Yurus raided our village, I never in a million years could have pictured the current situation, with me borderline bossing around one of their fiercest warriors.

He all but let himself drop on top of the stool in something akin to a tantrum. I once more bit the inside of my cheeks not to chuckle. I took the box from him and retrieved some gauze and their version of peroxide. On instinct, I stood in front of him, between his parted thighs. By default, Yurus always sat with their legs spread wider than human men, the three segments forming them no doubt making that position more comfortable for them.

As soon as I settled there, Wonjin lifted his hands before stiffening and putting them back down on his knees. My stomach did a backflip as I realized he'd almost placed them on my hips. He swallowed hard, and his floppy ears flicked a couple of times. That, too, made my innards do another somersault.

Dear God, why have I grown so irrationally attracted to this brutish pile of muscles?

And attracted, I truly was.

I still blamed Rihanna for planting the original seed. But I had to take ownership of allowing it to blossom and the fantasies that started playing in my mind of late, especially at night. Rihanna was tiny compared to her husband Zatruk. At five feet, barely a hundred and thirty pounds when wet to his seven feet and easily over three hundred pounds of pure muscles, how she managed to couple with him without getting split in half still boggled my mind. And yet, she was clearly very happy with her fluffy grump. Truth be told, I envied the way the terrifying leader of the Yurus turned into a complete puddle whenever he interacted with her.

Would Wonjin be this sweet with me?

The resounding 'yes' that resonated in my mind didn't help my cause. Forcing myself to focus on the task at hand, I poured some peroxide on the gauze before gently dabbing the cut on his forehead with it. The weight of Wonjin's dark eyes on me made me feel beyond self-conscious. The less I tried to pay attention to it, the more intensely I felt it.

"You're staring," I finally blurted out.

Wonjin lifted an eyebrow, the look on his face warning he was about to taunt me.

"Of course, I am. You're standing right in front of me, filling my entire field of vision," he replied matter-of-factly. "If I lower my gaze, I'll be staring at your breasts, which I'm sure you wouldn't approve of."

I inhaled sharply and glared at him for a second, robbed of words. He had a point. But the smugness of his discreet smirk made me want to smack him.

"I can avert my eyes if you feel intimidated. However, you might take offense and assume I dislike looking at you," he continued, a hint of dare slipping into his voice.

"I wouldn't think that," I mumbled with a frown.

"Is that what you would like me to do then? Avert my eyes and not look at you?" he insisted.

This time, the playfulness had left his voice. The subtle tension that replaced it implied my response actually mattered to him. Before Rihanna mentioned Wonjin's possible infatuation with me, such a detail would have flown a thousand feet over my head. I was the clueless type when it came to noticing when people had a crush on me. Usually, a man had to all but hold a neon sign pointing at me and shout his feelings through a bull-horn for me to get it.

In this instance, my gut was telling me Wonjin wanted to know whether his interest displeased me.

"No. I... I don't mind you looking at me," I whispered.

"You don't *mind*, but would you *prefer* I didn't?" he further insisted.

"If I didn't want you looking at me, I would have said as much. You can look all you want... If you want."

The expression that settled over his features messed me up. Our eyes locked, and the dark depths of his gaze seemed to draw me in, swallowing me whole. My skin tingled, and the sudden urge to lean forward and kiss his plump lips surged within me with a violence that left me reeling. A lock of his brown hair falling on his forehead and brushing over the wound I'd just cleaned snapped me out of my daze.

With the magic broken, I blinked and turned away from him to place the soiled gauze on the workbench and grab a bandage. Before I could even begin to unwrap it, a savage growl rose from his throat. Stunned, I froze and glanced at him.

"You will *not* put a bandage on me, woman," he ground through his teeth.

"But—"

"No. Bandages."

The finality in his tone and the hard glint in his eyes made it clear this wasn't open to discussion. It wasn't that big of a cut and didn't really need a bandage. I almost asked why, then it dawned on me. Yurus males took great pride in their strength and battle prowess. They flaunted their battle scars like trophies. To be seen walking around with a bandage over such a small scratch would have his clanmates mocking him as a weakling. Considering how much he'd been bullied in the past, I could see why he'd refused so categorically to give anyone grounds to make fun of him again.

"Fine," I mumbled. "But let me fix that lock of hair so it doesn't rub all over it."

Wonjin instantly relaxed and grunted his assent. My stomach fluttered as I reached for the wavy lock of hair and tucked it back under the single braid he'd bound the upper half of his hair with. The lower half hung loosely to his shoulders, framing his bushy beard, also adorned with two small braids.

"Your hair is really soft," I mused out loud, annoyed by my treacherous mouth revealing my thoughts.

Wonjin puffed out his chest. "Unlike some of the other idiots out there, I properly groom my hair and fur, and I don't needlessly soil them."

I snorted. Some of the male Yurus occasionally tended to be

a little unkempt, wiping their hands on their fur when eating.

"So I see," I replied, fighting the urge to run my fingers to the silky strands at the back of his head, just below his horns.

"You can touch," Wonjin said, as if he'd read the thoughts crossing my mind. "Go on."

I licked my lips nervously and complied. Dear God! It was beyond soft. I wanted to bury my face in his hair and rub against it. Wonjin's lips parted, his dark eyes smoldering as my hand glided down to his shoulder to rub over the fluffy patch of fur there. Realizing how bold I'd become, I jerked my hand away. Lightning fast, Wonjin caught my wrist with his left hand and placed my palm right back on his shoulder, his gaze heating further.

"Don't stop. I'm happy to help you sate whatever curiosity you may have about me or my people," Wonjin said, his deep voice seeming to have dipped another octave.

To my dismay, my mind took an instantaneous dive into the gutter upon hearing those words. Curious? Yes, I was curious. And my eyes made it clear where the main source of my curiosity lay when they flicked down and zeroed in on his crotch.

His audible gasp had my head jerking right back up, even as my cheeks felt on the verge of bursting into flames. Although his ears flapped, his face didn't take on its usual embarrassed expression.

"Well, I think we're done here," I said, mortified.

I turned away to put distance between us and tried to free my wrist from his hold. But Wonjin not only held firm, he rose to his feet. Towering over me by a good head, he stared at me with an intensity that had my knees feeling wobbly.

"Are we, Lara? Are we done?" he asked, a challenge in his voice.

I opened and closed my mouth a few times, any coherent thought I might form having apparently decided now was the time to take an extended leave of absence. My breath hitched in my throat when, still holding my palm pressed to his shoulder, Wonjin slipped an arm around my waist and drew me against his muscular body.

The oddest mix of desire, wariness, and determination played over his features as he studied my reaction to his bold move.

"Tell me to release you, and I will," he said, his voice so thick and rumbling, his chest vibrated against mine.

My still half-frozen brain was telling me now would be a good time to make a decision. At a visceral level, I understood that whatever would happen in the next seconds would forever change the course of my relationship with Wonjin. Was I ready to cross that line?

When I failed to say anything, his gaze darkened further, and his arm around me tightened its embrace, holding me even more closely against his firm body.

"I want to kiss you, Lara. Do you consent?"

A bolt of desire exploded in the pit of my stomach, sending fiery tendrils coursing through my veins. My eyes locked on his plush lips and the small pair of pristine tusks framing his mouth. My own lips parted in anticipation while my pulse picked up. I placed my free hand on his other shoulder, waiting for him to proceed.

Instead, he slightly frowned, his face taking on a stern expression. "Do you consent, Lara?" he repeated, this time more forcefully.

I realized then that he wouldn't kiss me—and would likely release me—if I didn't verbally state my agreement.

"Yes," I breathed out, my stomach fluttering, and my nipples hardening.

A triumphant—almost predatory—smile settled on his lips while his hand holding my palm to his left shoulder glided the length of my arm in a gentle caress before wrapping around my nape. His hand was so big, he could easily crush my neck like one would crumple a piece of paper. And yet, far from frightening me, it turned me on something fierce. To be at the mercy of such a powerful male who handled you with extreme care and respect was insanely thrilling.

Wonjin lowered his head. Eyes locked with mine, he lightly brushed my lips with his, studying my reactions. I leaned into him, pressing my mouth against his. I felt him smile in response. His hold tightened further as he took control of the kiss. Wonjin didn't try to deepen it right away, content to apply some pressure, as if to allow me to familiarize myself with the feel of his tusks. Far from awkward, it actually felt nice and even added a slight sense of thrill and of the forbidden.

His mouth then moved away from mine, gliding over my jawline, down to my neck, and then back up towards my earlobe. A rumbling purr of approval vibrated through his broad chest when I shivered in his arms. That spot right behind my ear was super sensitive. He sucked on my earlobe, nipping at it before lifting his head to look at me. The possessiveness in his gaze made me weak in the knees.

For a split second, I thought he was going to say something. Instead, he kissed me again, this time, his tongue invading my mouth like a conqueror. A bolt of fire exploded in the pit of my stomach, and a dull throbbing awakened between my thighs. I slipped one hand in his hair, while the other caressed a path down his insanely muscular chest and side, before wrapping around his back. Good God, his body was perfection. The furless patches of skin were as soft as a human's. Feeling him shiver in turn under my touch gave me the most insane sense of power.

Emboldened by my reaction, Wonjin's own touch grew more daring, his hand caressing my back in a downward journey before settling on my behind. He didn't just give my right cheek a squeeze, he grabbed it, held on to it, then pressed my pelvis against his.

His mouth swallowed my gasp when I felt his quickly hardening shaft between us. Despite my clothes and his loincloth, I could feel his massive club starting to push against my stomach. I normally took great pride in my cool and poise. But this had me pulling out from his embrace, taking a step back, and then gaping like a fish at his groin. Although I obviously couldn't see anything behind the thick, leather-like fabric, I stared as if I expected a boa to jump out of there.

More like an anaconda...

It was Wonjin's turn to gasp, drawing my gaze back up to his face while my cheeks burned like a thousand fires.

"Avert your eyes, woman. I am not showing you my cock. First, you should at least have asked me for an intimate walk in the woods, or those romantic dinners humans are apparently fond of in the 'get-to-know-you' phase," he said, sounding outraged. "And second, you didn't even claim me! I am deeply offended."

"No, I… It's not… I didn't…"

Words failed me as I struggled to find an appropriate response. I certainly couldn't explain to him that feeling his humongous cock between us had me instantly fearing I'd get split in half trying to ride him. But then, that *did* imply I assumed he would *agree* to roll in the hay with me. More disturbing still, it also hinted to the fact *I* was thinking about taking it there.

To my shock, Wonjin's apparent outrage faded as quickly as it had flared. His face melted in a soft, almost taunting smile as a chuckle tumbled out of his throat. I stared in disbelief as I finally realized he'd been teasing me. He carefully drew me back against his body, and I went willingly, too shocked to react other-wise—aside from wanting to kick his butt.

"Do not fear me, or anything about me, my Lara," Wonjin said in a soft, but serious voice. "There is no rush between us. When the time comes, I will take great care of you. If nothing else, Great Chieftain Zatruk and Rihanna are the proof that a human and a Yurus can harmoniously come together. You were made for me, and I for you. I claim you as my woman."

My skin felt hot and cold all at once, while my brain was

getting a bit of a whiplash. Since my wretched mouth had a mind of its own—usually a sassy or sarcastic one—it defaulted to its usual defense mechanism when my brain didn't react quickly enough.

"*When* that time comes?" I repeated. "You're assuming it *will* come."

The words no sooner left my lips than I inwardly kicked myself. I had not come here looking to start a relationship, but now that he was making his move, the idea was definitely growing on me.

Totally unfazed, Wonjin leaned forward, his hands tightening around my waist while his black eyes bore into mine. "Are you challenging my claim, Lara?"

I scrunched my face and mumbled something unintelligible.

"That wasn't an answer. I asked you a question. Are you challenging my claim?" he insisted, more sternly.

This time, I gave him an annoyed look. "What's with you and insisting on clear answers?" I asked, aggravated by the whiny edge in my voice.

"Because when it comes to a female's consent, there should never be any doubt," he said, this time all playfulness gone. "I want you to be mine, and I want you to claim me. If you do not wish to have me, state so now."

For some dumb reason, my stupid mouth wouldn't just agree and had to continue being difficult. "What if I say no?"

To my surprise, he didn't appear hurt or upset. Wonjin simply shrugged, a smug expression on his face. "You won't say no. If that had been your intention, you would have said as much already. And you wouldn't still be in my embrace with your arms around my waist."

My eyes widened in shock as I realized I indeed had my arms around him and was leaning against his firm body. I couldn't recall doing any of that.

"But to answer your question—as I practice what I ask of

others—if you said no, I would simply go on wooing and pursuing you until you gave in. You are mine, and I am yours. You might as well spare us both the headache and just give in," he stated, matter-of-factly.

I burst out laughing, while shaking my head at him in disbelief. Normally, overconfident—not to say arrogant—people rubbed me the wrong way. I could become quite contrarian specifically to spite them or take them down a notch. But Wonjin's ballsy assertion had my toes curling instead. The subtle underlying shyness in his eyes undoubtedly played a part in my response.

"When you put it in such a romantic fashion, how could I say no?" I replied mockingly.

"You can't," he deadpanned. "Are you mine, Lara?"

"I don't know. What does that entail?" I asked, once more wondering why I was dragging things on, knowing the answer was already yes.

"It entails me hugging and kissing you whenever I please, spoiling you even when you argue about it for no good reason other than your strange human principles, and spending time with you other than to work on Zatruk's project. It also means you granting me the right to crack the skull of any male who dares challenge my claim on you."

I snorted. "I knew there would be some skull cracking involved in there somewhere."

"Of course!" he retorted proudly. However, his grin faded almost instantly, a serious expression settling on his features. "Does it bother you that we fight?"

I took a second to reflect on my answer, which had him immediately looking worried. Smiling reassuringly, I rubbed my palm on his chest in a way I hoped would be soothing for him.

"Now that I understand that it is a physiological need for males of your species to fight regularly, it no longer bothers me," I replied in all sincerity. "But you Yurus are so damn strong, I can't help being scared for you at times. The type of blows you guys exchange during those brawls would shatter the bones of a human. It's unnerving."

The huge smile that stretched his lips messed with my head. Wonjin normally only had three expressions: unimpressed grumpiness, stern scowl, or 'I'm-about-to-tear-you-limb-from-limb' feral look. Well, if we excluded his embarrassed air while his floppy ears flicked like a butterfly's wings... But this soft and happy look on his face, knowing that only I could put it on there, I could definitely get used to.

"You worry for my welfare, my mate," he said smugly. "I knew you cared. But there is no need. It will take far more than a mere brawl for me to get injured. Now claim me, woman."

"So bossy," I mumbled, scrunching my face at him. "Fine, you bully. I claim you. But don't you use me as an excuse to go smack your friends around."

"I don't need excuses for that," he said triumphantly, before lifting me up.

I yelped, my legs instinctively wrapping around his waist and my palms clinging onto his broad shoulders. Whatever words I'd intended to say, he swallowed with a greedy kiss. The dull throbbing between my thighs came back with a vengeance as Wonjin's tongue plundered my mouth. Despite the obvious control he was exerting, I could feel the passion burning inside him, itching to be set free.

A moan rose in my throat as his right hand settled on my behind, caressing it with a possessiveness and an urgency that had my inner walls contracting with need. Good heavens, how the heck was he getting me hot and bothered so quickly? Even as our tongues warred with each other, I felt his shaft hardening once more against my stomach. This time, I didn't panic or shy away. Instead, I pushed my pelvis forward and started grinding against him while my hands roamed over his muscular body.

To my shock, Wonjin abruptly ended the kiss. He yanked his

head back with an almost angry growl that resonated straight in my core and had my nipples instantly hardening. He fisted my hair at my nape, holding my head in front of his while he stared at me with a feral expression that had moisture pooling between my thighs. His nostrils flared, and his chest vibrated with another growl. That Wonjin could smell my arousal didn't even embarrass me. Right this instant, I was feeling so damn horny, I wanted him to slam my back on top of his workbench and then for him to fuck me into next week.

That didn't even make sense considering how fairly prudish I usually acted.

Eyes locked with mine, looking like he wanted to savage me in unspeakable ways, Wonjin started walking. A bolt of lust exploded in the pit of my stomach, and my skin heated with the thrill of anticipation and an irrational desire for him to ravage me. But at the back of my head, a little panicked voice was telling me to slow things down. This was too quick, too soon. We didn't fuck on the first date. Heck, we hadn't even had a date to begin with!

And yet, my stupid mouth chose that moment not to randomly express itself. I remained quiet, my inner walls contracting spasmodically with the need to be filled.

"You're a hazard, female," Wonjin grumbled, his voice so gravelly with desire his words were almost unintelligible. "But you will not lure me into temptation… just yet."

It took a moment for my brain to comprehend the meaning of his words. Only once he stopped walking did it finally register he hadn't been heading towards the door connecting to the rest of his house. Instead, he'd headed towards the door leading outside then put me back on my feet.

Speechless, I gaped at him as he opened the door and gestured for me to exit.

"I'm taking you out on a date," he said with his usual grumpy tone.

CHAPTER 4
WONJIN

An inferno raged in my loins as I waited for my woman to exit my forge. By the baffled expression on her beautiful face, Lara didn't understand why I was taking her outside rather than to my bedchamber. The Ancestors knew I wanted nothing more than to do just that. Even now, I had to call upon every shred of my willpower not to toss her over my shoulder and carry her to my room to have my unbridled way with her. But she needed to know that true, deep feelings stirred me where she was concerned, not just lust. I would properly woo her before surrendering to the burning passion she awakened in me.

Lara was mine, my woman… my mate.

I still couldn't believe she had consented to be mine and claimed me as hers. From the moment I'd laid eyes on her, Lara had set my blood ablaze. I'd never ached or hungered for a female as much as I did her. It made even less sense that, before her, I'd never thought of human women as particularly attractive.

The first time I'd seen a human, I'd thought they were mutants or horribly disfigured creatures. Their straight legs had looked wonky to me. The grace with which they nonetheless managed to walk with them made me realize back then that it wasn't actually a deformity.

They were scrawny, physically weak, without fur, horns, or a tail, all elements that contributed to a Yurus' attractiveness. The size and shine on the hooves of a Yurus revealed a lot about their health and the strength of their bloodline. Thick hooves, wider around the base, and with a perfectly centered cleft were guaranteed to draw many admiring glances. But humans walked on an odd, altered version of their hands, which they called feet, with short fingers named toes.

My initial horror at such a sight had waned over the years, slowly shifting into indifference. But now, I found them rather adorable, especially on my woman. Lara often wore open feet coverings humans referred to as sandals. Considering the hot weather that we enjoyed almost year-round on Cibbos, it made sense they would protect their fragile feet with coverings that weren't too warm. Lara's feet were delicate, her toes dainty and often ornate with pretty colors on the nails. When she was focused or reflecting on a problem, she wiggled them in the cutest fashion, the big toes perking up and staying up when she suddenly got struck by a great idea.

As soon as Lara exited the forge, I followed her out and closed the door behind me. I gazed at her beautiful face, fighting the urge to kiss her again. She was looking at me with a confused expression. The lingering scent of her arousal needled me to reconsider my plan.

"I'm taking you out on a date," I explained, annoyed by my tone. "I do not trust myself not to get carried away if we remain inside my dwelling."

Like most Yurus males, I spoke in a way that often sounded belligerent. I didn't mean to. It just came out that way. The term 'date' constituted one of the many things that made little sense when it came to human terminology. Date meant a specific day in a calendar. Why had they turned this into meaning private time with your partner?

Lara blinked. Her surprise gave way to something akin to shyness as she smiled at me. My heart swelled: my woman approved of my course of action.

"A date, uh? Okay. Where to? And weren't you supposed to show me the speeder?" Lara asked.

"Yes, a date in my favorite place to spend quiet time by myself. The speeder can wait. You are too tempting for us to linger here safely," I replied while taking her hand.

It felt so fragile in my much bigger hand, instantly stirring my protective instincts. The way she trustingly closed her small fingers around it did pleasant things to me. Yurus didn't walk hand in hand with their mates. We didn't have a problem with public displays of affection, but it was mostly limited to our females sitting in our lap during shared meals in the town square.

The short walk to the stables required us to stroll past the square... where my clanmates were still fighting. A different set of pugilists were at it—some of the previous brawlers now standing on the sidelines cheering them on. Clearly, the original fight I'd partaken in had ended and a new one had begun over yet another silly reason.

Seeing Gulkis land a solid punch on Tarmek's obnoxious face had my lips quirking up in an almost malicious grin. Hearing Lara huff in discouragement wiped it out. I cast a worried glance her way. Relief flooded through me upon realizing it was my clanmates fighting that had prompted her reaction, and not my delight at seeing my former bully getting roughed up. She shook her head at the males like one does when faced with a hopeless case.

Although my Lara had claimed she understood why we Yurus needed to fight, worry gnawed at me that she would eventually tire of us doing it. Brawling wasn't just a physiological need for Yurus males, for me, it was a real addiction. I *loved* fighting. Even back when my clanmates abused my injury, I couldn't get enough of fighting. Now that Luana—the doctor from the human colony—had healed me, I obsessed with it even more. Years of holding my own in combat even with a disability had made me a formidable opponent. Now that I no longer suffered from that handicap, few dared to challenge me. Even Tarmek—who had been deemed Great Chieftain Zatruk's only potential competition—now steered clear of me.

I shuddered at the prospect that this could become an issue.

The gawkers turning to stare at Lara and me swept those grim thoughts away. Even the brawlers gradually stopped fighting to gape at us, the scene eerily similar to the first day Zatruk brought his mate Rihanna into Mutarak.

Even as I puffed out my chest with pride a terrible thought crossed my mind. My eyes flicked towards my mate to assess her reaction to our brand-new relationship thus being exposed to the world. Would she be embarrassed? Self-conscious? Would she…?

A single glance at her gorgeous face had my heart swelling to bursting. Lifting her pointy chin with an air of defiance, my Lara tightened her hold around my hand, as if daring anyone to challenge her claim on me. The pride I felt at calling this human mine and to have been claimed by her went into overdrive. I bunched my muscles to appear more imposing and stomped my hooves to give my gait maximum swagger. I even flicked my tail left and right on a wide radius in a boastful display.

As we walked past the stunned crowd, I made eye contact with as many males as possible, both daring them to challenge me and showing off how I, Wonjin, had earned the affection of a female they held no chance of ever sparking her interest.

Movement at the edge of the crowd caught my attention. My chest warmed with love upon recognizing my mother. Both of her palms pressed to her chest, she was staring at us with an almost teary smile, her joy for me plain for all to see. I had made no secrets to her about my feelings for Lara. Mother had been convinced I could win her over, but I had completely doubted it. Even though I knew better, after decades of my clanmates constantly repeating that I was an idiot and too damaged to ever earn the love of a worthy female, I had started to believe it.

It had not helped that the first time I had met her, Lara had hardly spared me a glance. Granted, she'd been fascinated by the speeder we had brought to the colony of Kastan in the hopes one of the human engineers could help us solve some design issues.

As much as they respected me intellectually, our own females had never considered me as a potential mate because of my previous injury. They had feared any offspring we might have would have been weak and damaged. It was only since Luana healed me that they suddenly started pursuing me. But Lara had already captured my heart.

Ancestors, I still couldn't believe she was mine.

Although we could have walked to my 'secret lair' right outside the city walls, I led my mate to the stables.

"No, you are riding with me," I said in a stern voice when she started heading towards her zeebis.

By the look she gave me, Lara wasn't too keen on me "bossing her around" like Rihanna liked to say.

"I'm fluffy. You'll be a lot more comfy with me," I added, my stupid ears flicking again.

Referring to myself in those completely absurd terms was an embarrassment in and of itself. But Rihanna often used it with her mate as something very positive.

After soundly humbling me on the day of her arrival in Mutarak, our Clan Mistress had shown me an unexpected kindness, going so far as adopting me as her little brother, even though I was far bigger and older than she was. For the first time in ages, she had made me feel like I mattered, that I was smart, and that I had much to offer. Granted, my mother always said as much, but that was her duty. Rihanna had truly become the sister of my heart. Her getting Luana to heal me sealed the deal.

So I had no qualms following her suggestions or her lead. And once again, that proved wise. I no sooner finished speaking those silly words than Lara's frown faded. An amused expression settled on her features as she gave me a slow once over.

Ancestors, I loved the possessive way in which she let her gaze roam over me in a slow caress.

"When you put it that way, it's hard to resist. You *are* rather fluffy," Lara conceded with a smile in her voice.

I silenced an inner groan at this failure of my own doing. My mate should deem me fierce, intimidating, and fearsome. Not fluffy.

After I carefully lifted my Lara to place her on Cilo, I climbed behind her. She leaned back against me, and I wrapped a possessive arm around her. I made no effort to swallow back the purr that rose in my throat.

Ancestors, she felt so good in my arms!

"Yep, very comfy!" she added with a giggle.

She pressed herself further against my chest while resting a hand on my arm holding her. My heart swelled, and I gently rubbed my cheek against hers, marking her with my scent.

I wanted to pinch myself to make sure this wasn't just another of my wishful fantasies of finally claiming Lara. This morning, as I prepared to show her the speeder, I'd been trying to come up with an excuse to delay when it would be completed or to find something new we could work on jointly together. As work on the battle arena would soon begin, I would have had no more opportunities to spend time with her and hopefully make her finally see me. Never in a thousand years did I expect this turn of events.

We rode at a snail's pace out of Mutarak and down the path to the pond located at a ten-minute walk from the city walls. A part of me wanted to ride farther into the woods instead to prolong this pleasant ride. Another slightly worried at the fact that I hadn't properly planned this outing. I liked things organized. So this impromptu date was not only nothing like my usual behavior but also revealed how overwhelmed I had felt.

I wanted Lara to like me. Correction: I wanted Lara to fall in love with me. Therefore, I needed to do everything right—number one by showing her respect and restraint. But human ways still confounded me, despite all the reading I had done on the subject of late. Her horrified reaction at the Moon Hawk I had gifted her still stung. Rihanna had explained to me later that such an offering didn't mean anything to humans. Lara had further tried to soothe the wound by bringing me a piece of the cooked Hawk. But you didn't have to be a genius to see that although she had appreciated the gesture, it didn't mean much to her.

"So what's this place you're taking me to?" Lara asked.

"We call it the pond, although shallow lake would probably be more accurate," I replied as we approached the clearing leading to it. "Growing up, I would spend hours, sometimes the entire day there."

"Really? Doing what?" she asked with genuine curiosity.

"Everything from reading, studying, swimming, fishing, or polishing my weapons," I replied, holding back the part about heavy daydreaming.

She opened her mouth to ask a question, then stopped herself, biting her bottom lip instead.

"What were you going to ask? You can speak freely," I said in a gentle tone.

"I... hmmm..."

"Let me guess," I said when her voice trailed off. "You were going to ask me if I came here alone or if I ever wanted to play with the other younglings. Am I correct?"

I smiled when the reddening of her face confirmed my suspicions.

"Remember that I claimed you as my woman, and you claimed me as yours," I gently chastised her. "That means you can freely ask me any question. For this to work, we must be able to discuss any topic and openly share our thoughts with each other without fear."

"You're right," she said sheepishly. "But I know you were injured before. I don't want to upset you if it's still a sore topic."

"The hardships I endured because of that injury will always be a sore memory for me, but they do not define me. Learning to live with it and overcoming that challenge are what made me who I am," I said factually. "I do not mind discussing it."

Leaning back sideways, Lara looked at me over her shoulder with an approving glimmer that made me want to purr.

"That's a good way to approach it," Lara said. "But yes, those were the general questions I wanted to ask."

I grunted. "No other younglings hung out with me. This place was both my playground and my refuge."

The trees parted before us revealing the stunning oasis that remained my sacred haven. The large pond with crystalline water stretched on over close to three hundred meters. Extensive patches of grass all around had afforded plenty of room for me to run around as a child, sheltered by the privacy offered by the tree line. A few berry bushes nearby—most of which I had planted growing up—had provided me with light snacks when I couldn't be bothered to fish or cook.

"This is beautiful," Lara breathed out as I stopped Cilo by the trees.

"I'm glad you like it," I grumbled, my stupid grumpy tone resurfacing as soon as I started feeling self-conscious again.

It made no sense considering she wasn't judging me but a natural setting. Still, it was my special place. And had she found it lacking, I would have undoubtedly taken it personally.

I helped her down and led her by the hand to give her the tour.

"As you probably noticed, Yurus don't really leave the city walls except to hunt," I explained as we walked alongside the water. "As there is no prey here, nobody bothers with this area. When I would get bullied too much, if I needed some time to heal from a particularly brutal defeat, or if I just wanted some peace, I would come here," I said wistfully.

"I'm so sorry," Lara said, her eyes filled with commiseration.

I snorted. "There's no need to be," I said, amused. "Truth be told, I initiated many of those fights where I ended up getting spanked. I love fighting. But I also love reading, which wasn't well-received by the others. While mentalities are finally changing, the pursuit of advanced academic studies made the others question whether eating praxilla leaves had not only caused my deformity but also emasculated me. Among my people, only females study sciences."

"Whoa. That's crazy," Lara said, shocked. "Praxilla are those leaves the Yurus males eat to control your bloodlust, right?"

I nodded. "Yes. That's also what caused the bone spurs that plagued my existence. I started consuming it too early. We should have waited until after puberty once my bones were properly set. But I do not regret being the test subject for it. Without that, I would have turned like all the others and never discovered the beauty of science and knowledge."

"Man, you really are something else! Young boys in Kastan who find a hiding place certainly don't spend their time learning physics just for fun," Lara said in a teasing tone, although genuine admiration shone in her dark eyes.

I chuckled. "My mother is our clan's Head Scientist. Libraries do not abound in Mutarak. So what reading material I could get mostly came from her. Later on, I would get everything I could on every possible topic from the smugglers who illegally dropped by Cibbos in violation of the Prime Directive and… during raids in your village," I added sheepishly.

Lara's jaw dropped. She obviously hadn't expected such a

confession from me. I couldn't even believe I'd admitted this to her, at least not this early in our relationship.

"Your clanmates pillaged our food, and you pillaged our books?" she asked, incredulous.

My wretched ears started flipping while my skin heated. "We couldn't really fight humans. Your people are too fragile. There is no pleasure—or honor for that matter—in fighting or terrorizing an opponent who is much weaker. Since our former Great Chieftain Vyrax demanded we join the raids, I went after the prize that made the most sense to me," I added with a shrug, inwardly kicking myself for bringing this up.

"A book thief... I had not seen that one coming," Lara said teasingly.

I grunted before leading her to the series of berry bushes and fruit trees on the east side of the pond. "It was actually from those books that I learned which fruits to grow here and how best to tend to them. The Yurus do not farm. We hunt and forage, which is why we are so grateful for the trade agreement Zatruk negotiated with your leader."

"That explains it! I thought it was incredibly strange to see this mix of trees and bushes growing together in this area," Lara said, impressed. "So, you're a master blacksmith, a brilliant aeronautical engineer, *and* an agricultural savant."

"Hardly a savant, but I am respectably knowledgeable in that field. However, I am well-versed in many more fields, including medicine, biochemistry, and pharmacology," I said proudly.

I puffed out my chest some more at the bewildered look Lara gave me.

"You're not old enough to know all that!" she exclaimed.

I burst out laughing. "You underestimate how much time I've had on my hands. Aside from being very curious, some of my studies were self-serving. With my mother's help, I tried for many years to find a cure to my illness."

"Right, that makes sense," Lara conceded, although she continued to gaze at me with awe.

As much as I wanted to continue basking in her admiration, this 'date' couldn't just be about me bragging.

"I hope you are a little hungry. I want you to try one of my favorite treats," I said.

"Not hungry per se, but I wouldn't mind a snack," she said, looking intrigued.

"Stand right here," I said with a grin. "And watch your head. You don't want to get knocked unconscious by a pika nut."

Her eyes bulged. "By a what?"

"You'll see!"

With this I hurried to the tall pika tree located just a few meters away. Its long, sagging fronds did wonders hiding the thick, round, and hard-shelled fruits it produced. The naturally spiky bark of the tree gave my hooves enough purchase to allow me to climb it with relative ease.

"Be careful!" Lara exclaimed, as I kept going up.

A part of me wanted to feel offended she would fear I might fall, as if I would be so clumsy. But once again, I was too busy reveling in the genuine concern she felt for my welfare. To think I'd been all but a ghost to her for so many weeks.

I glanced down at her over my shoulder. She looked even smaller and more fragile from this vantage point. I'd only climbed four meters and still had at least another three to go before I could reach my prize.

"Do not worry, my mate. I'm fine," I said with a smug grin before resuming my ascent.

Moments later, the massive fronds of the tree closed all around me, shielding me from view. It felt cooler in the shade but also got my adrenaline pumping. Some nasty critters often built their nests in the darkness the fronds provided. Getting half my face bitten off by a blasiq snake and falling off the tree in front of my brand-new mate didn't feature too high on my to do list. With the high density of my bones, such a fall wouldn't damage me, merely stun me for a moment. The injury I'd never recover from would be the humiliation of crash landing in front of Lara.

Thankfully, I regularly used high-frequency whistles around the tree, which kept the snakes from trying to settle there as the sound was highly grating to their sensitive ears. To my delight, large pika nuts awaited me. I had worried they could still be too small or not ripe enough. But the honeyed scent that emanated from them confirmed they would be perfectly sweet.

I had initially planned on tossing down a couple of them before bringing another pair down with me, but these nuts were massive enough that a single one would make an ample portion for one person. I grabbed a nut in each hand, my fingers barely long enough to wrap around half of each. Pressing the nuts against the spiky bark of the tree to protect my palms, I prepared to return to my mate.

"Coming down!" I shouted over my shoulder.

I turned my ankles to the side so the flat of my hooves would rest against the trunk then loosened my grip, allowing gravity to work its magic. My weight immediately dragged me down as I slid the length of the tree in seconds. I repressed a laugh at Lara's frightened shout. From where she stood, I probably looked like I'd lost my grip. For me, it was a much too brief thrill ride. A slightly burnt scent tickled my nose as I jumped down from the tree, seconds before I would have hit the ground. I landed gracefully on my hooves before turning to face my mate with a smug expression. Mouth gaping, she stared in turn at me then at the tree before frowning disapprovingly at me.

"You scared me! I thought you were falling!" Lara scolded.

"You have too little faith in me, my mate," I retorted with a grin. "I merely glided down."

"Those spikes could have shredded your skin to hell and back!" she argued.

"They *would* have had I not taken the proper precautions beforehand," I said teasingly before showing the massive nuts. "See that skid mark on the shell? That's what rubbed against the bark, not my skin."

Lara looked at the nuts. Although she appeared somewhat mollified, she still scrunched her face at me. "You could have warned me," she mumbled.

"And miss this lovely display of your concern for me?" I replied with exaggerated shock. "Never, my Lara. I'm enjoying this way too much."

Leaning forward, I kissed the tip of her nose. She swatted me away, seeming unable to decide if she wanted to smile or kick me. Either course of action would suit me just fine.

"Stop pouting, little human. This treat is guaranteed to sweeten even the most sour of dispositions," I teased.

"You know, I think I like you more when you're grumpy than bratty," she muttered.

"You like me, period," I said with a confidence I couldn't explain.

Without giving her a chance to argue, I led her to the natural rock formation near a bush that served as both my secret vault and workstation. I activated the hidden latch. The entire front panel of the rock flipped open, revealing the waterproof cache where I stashed my tablet, fishing and cooking equipment, some tools, and utensils.

"Holy shit! That's so awesome!" Lara said, running a hand over the light, but sturdy hollowed rock that closed my safe.

"Thank you. It was a fun little engineering project my mother had tasked me with," I said proudly. "If you press here, this flat rock on top will rotate and serve as a table. I worked on many assignments right there growing up."

"Man, is there anything you can't do?" Lara asked, looking a bit overwhelmed.

"There are too many things I can't do," I confessed. "You do not want to hear me sing or perform those strange human dances. I can cook any meat or vegetable, but baking and pastry making confounds me. According to Rihanna, my sense of humor is beyond challenged, as are my diplomatic skills," I added with a shrug.

Lara snorted. "Now I really want to see you dance and hear you sing."

"That will *never* happen," I growled while taking out two spoons from my cache.

"Aww, come on! I'm sure it would be super cute."

Glaring at her, I picked up one of the nuts, pointed to the knot it originally attached to the tree from, and slammed it on top of the hard surface of the 'table.' It immediately fractured in half, the sweet scent of the fruit filling the air.

"I think it is best you eat before you make any other disturbing suggestions," I grumbled.

Sitting down on the rock by the table, I drew Lara into my lap. She came willingly, a glimmer of mischief shining bright in her eyes as she continued to stare at me, visibly itching to poke at me some more. While the thought of dancing for her horrified me, I loved that she was feeling sufficiently at ease to tease me.

"You know, singing love songs to your woman is one of the common courting rituals among humans, Lara taunted.

"I have read about human courtship," I countered, unfazed. "Playing audio recordings of the most famous romantic singers is an acceptable—and more common—approach. I have already identified a few pieces that could become *our* song."

Her eyes widened. "You have?"

I gave her a stiff nod. "Yes, I have. Now eat, woman."

I picked up one of the two halves of the pika nut and gave it to her. Lara lifted it to her nose, taking a cautious whiff. Relief flooded through me as she seemed pleasantly surprised by its aroma.

That she had needed to bring it this close to her face

reminded me how stunted some of the human senses were. For me, the scent permeated the air. My protective instincts instantly went into overdrive. I needed to keep my woman safe from all the things she couldn't see, hear, or smell and that could put her in danger.

"The shell looks like a pineapple and a coconut had a baby. But the filling looks like a thick pudding. What should I expect?" Lara asked, a slight worry audible in her voice.

"The meat is sweet and creamy," I said, pointing at the light-beige thick texture that filled the shell. "The dark spots you see are the seeds, which are fully edible. They are crunchy like nuts and add a pleasant bit of saltiness. Trust me."

Even as I spoke those words, I dipped the spoon inside the pika nut and scooped a bit of both the filling and the seeds. Lara licked her lips nervously as I brought the spoon before her face. Despite her wariness, she leaned forward. Instead of opening her mouth, my woman poked her tongue out to take a small lick at some of the cream. She tasted it, her lips smacking noisily, before her eyes widened in shock.

"Oh, my God! This tastes like walnut maple cheesecake and has the same texture!" Lara exclaimed.

To my utter surprise—and complete delight—Lara yanked the spoon out of my hand and dug in. She shoved a big spoonful into her mouth and started chewing. My skin heated and my blood rushed straight to my groin when Lara closed her eyes and emitted a deep and sexy moan as she savored the treat.

I stared at her in silence as she scarfed down three more big spoonfuls back-to-back. When she began licking the spoon, a bolt of lust surged within. Lara stopped, finally noticing me observing her.

"You're not eating?" she asked, suddenly looking self-conscious.

"In a moment. For now, I rather enjoy watching you eat," I said, my voice so deep I felt it vibrate through my chest.

I didn't know what expression I displayed, but if it reflected even a tenth of the burning desire I felt for my female, it would explain the redness creeping on her cheeks. Lara averted her eyes and pushed around the thick cream inside the nut with the tip of her spoon.

"It's really good," she whispered, almost apologetically.

"It is," I concurred, my gaze weighing heavily on her.

Lara gave me a nervous sideways glance then shifted in my lap. She stiffened after the second wiggle, the redness of her face cranking up another notch as she bit her bottom lip. I didn't need to ask what had prompted that reaction. My cock was so hard it hurt. I just wanted to rip the half-eaten pika nut out of her hand, throw it to the ground, toss her on top of the table, and unleash my passion on her.

But not on the first date.

Or the second... Or third...

My female swallowed hard, the most maddening mix of arousal and fear in her scent driving me insane.

"Eat, my Lara. You are safe with me," I said.

Although my words seemed to have the desired effect of lessening her wariness, the oddest expression flitted over her face.

"Maybe *you* are not safe with *me*," she whispered.

I stared at her, speechless.

With an incredible smugness, Lara turned to pick up a spoon on the stone table, stuck it in the other half of the pika nut, then extended it to me.

"It is rude to stare at people while they're eating. So, eat!" she ordered.

I complied.

CHAPTER 5
LARA

Dating a Yurus was nothing like I'd ever imagined. Rihanna had not been kidding by saying they were fluffy and cuddly. Wonjin certainly was the biggest and sweetest teddy bear I'd ever met. I still couldn't get over the fact that he once used to terrify me. Now, his mere presence in a room, even if he stood at the other end, made me feel safe. It was the gentle way in which he touched me like I was made of the finest crystal with those massive hands of his. The softness in his voice and the tender awe in his eyes whenever he addressed me made me feel worshiped.

Honestly, I didn't understand what he saw in me. I wasn't plain or ugly by any means, but men didn't fall all over themselves pursuing me either. Personality-wise, I often came across as dismissive or haughty. God knew it wasn't intentional. I just got so focused on things that the rest of the world pretty much ceased to exist. You could talk to me during that time and, while I'd hear your voice, your words would fly a thousand kilometers over my head. I'd just "uh-huh" you to death until you snapped at me for not listening. Only then would I realize I had indeed not been listening.

That never seemed to bother Wonjin. Whenever he found me in the zone, he usually left me alone until I remembered the world around me. If he truly needed my attention right there and then, he just picked me up in his arms or sat me in his lap. Should I protest or complain, he'd just silently stare at me until I stopped, then tell me what he wanted. I couldn't even get annoyed because the wretched male gave the best cuddles.

Yes, I was falling hard for my Minotaur.

When I took him home to meet my parents, I had dreaded the worst—not that it would have made me break things off. But my parents were extremely old school and very much aligned with the conservative mentality that had prompted the original settlers to leave Earth and move away from all its technology and return to more traditional ways. So their joy at finding out their only daughter, who they constantly feared would end up a spinster, finally found herself a boyfriend faded the minute they realized he was Yurus.

Walking into the house, Wonjin had to slightly bow his head so as not to hit the top of the doorframe. My father stood next to my mother, his sternest expression plastered all over his face as he gave Wonjin a less-than-subtle once over. I groaned inwardly while Mom just stood there with her usual neutral air.

"Wonjin, meet my parents, Haru and Mika Kimura," I said waving first at my father then at my mother. "Mom, Dad, this is Wonjin."

"Mister and Missis Kimura, it is a pleasure to meet you," Wonjin said in his most polite voice, for once devoid of the grumpy rumbling.

When silence met his greeting, I gave my parents a "What the fuck?!" look hoping they wouldn't humiliate our entire family like this by offending my boyfriend who also happened to be their guest.

"You are not exactly what I expected my daughter to bring home as her partner," Dad said at last.

"Dad!" I exclaimed, feeling both shocked and outraged by such rudeness.

"It's okay, my Lara," Wonjin said in an appeasing tone. "He's merely being honest. I never expected I would be taken by a human, just like I doubt you ever thought you'd end up with a Yurus."

"Expectations are irrelevant," I said sternly. "All that matters is that I ended up with a nice guy who I really like."

To my dismay, instead of chastising my father, as I had intended, my words set Wonjin's ears into their telltale frantic flapping.

"Why are your ears flicking?" Mother asked, scrunching her face as she stared at them.

Fuck my life! I wished the ground would open and swallow me whole. What a bad idea this had been. The flicking of Wonjin's ears went into overdrive. I was opening my mouth to say maybe it was best we leave when Wonjin responded to my mother.

"It is a nervous tick that usually triggers when I'm feeling embarrassed or, in this instance, self-conscious," Wonjin said matter-of-factly.

I stared at him in shock at that confession, the feeling reflected on my parents' faces.

"Why are you feeling self-conscious?" Dad asked, this time with genuine curiosity.

"Because I'm madly in love with your daughter, and I don't want to embarrass her in front of her family. She respects and values your opinion. I'm well-aware you would have wanted someone different from her, but you will never find a male who will cherish, protect, and respect her more than I will."

Under different circumstances, I would have laughed at the way my parents gaped at him. But I was too busy melting from the inside out. I slipped my hand into Wonjin's. He turned his head to look at me. The minute our gazes connected, the world faded around us. Whatever doubt might have lingered at the back of my mind vanished in that instant. Although it was still early in our relationship, I knew at a visceral level that I'd found the one.

Dad clearing his throat broke the magic. "Well, my wife didn't spend all day cooking just so that we would let it grow cold while standing at the entrance. Come in."

For the first time, I realized his stern tone in many ways reminded me of Wonjin. When embarrassed or trying to hide his softer side, Dad would often become grumpy or act annoyed. Wonjin's words about me had touched him. But my wretched father would never admit it.

As soon as we settled at the table, Dad unleashed the full Inquisition on him. He questioned him on everything from his entire lineage, including the professions of his parents, to his own education level and hobbies, down to proving his ability to provide for our eventual family, since the Yurus didn't have any real currency. I was beyond mortified. But Wonjin couldn't look less unbothered, answering each question directly and succinctly. Mom had to intervene a couple of times so that my poor boyfriend could have a second to take a bite before the meal went cold.

Being an engineer himself, Dad started testing Wonjin's knowledge with trick questions. Before long, my man—well my Yurus—was running circles around Dad. He was insanely smart. His analytical mind never ceased to amaze me. Behind his rough and sometimes almost brutish demeanor, he was a silent force to be reckoned with. Even my mom was giving him approving glances. The fact that he devoured her food and clearly enjoyed all of it earned him a heck of a lot of extra brownie points.

By the time dinner ended, Dad and Wonjin were having animated discussions about physics principles and their aeronautical applications as if they were planning on building their own interstellar ship.

"Well, we should probably head out," I said at last when Dad looked nowhere near ready to stop talking.

"Yes," Wonjin said, looking surprised at the time. "The sun will set soon. We must hurry if we do not wish to be late."

The goodbyes were leaps and bounds warmer than the welcome had been.

"Next time you come, I'll make some korokke for you," Mother said to Wonjin.

"*And* tebasaki!" my father added enthusiastically. "You must try my wife's tebasaki. It's the best chicken you will have in all of Kastan, not to say all of Cibbos."

My throat tightened with emotion. This second invitation was my parents' way of giving their blessing to our relationship. Although I wouldn't have ended things with Wonjin even if they had disapproved, their support meant the world to me. By the way Wonjin's ears flicked a couple of times, he had understood it as well.

"I look forward to enjoying your wonderful cooking again," he replied politely.

"Mmhmm. We need you well-fed if you are to give my daughter strong babies," Mom added.

My cheeks all but burst into flames while Wonjin's ears seemed like they were trying to fly him away from this situation. Dad looked like he couldn't decide if he wanted to be amused by Wonjin's display of embarrassment or annoyed at his wife for already talking babies at this early stage. The worst part was that, now that my father had deemed my boyfriend acceptable, he was worried Mom would scare him away with such topics.

"We really have to go," I said while glaring at my mother, who smiled at me with an overly innocent expression that fooled no one. "Thanks for the great meal. I'll see you later."

Wonjin mumbled a farewell and led me hastily to the wicked speeder he had built for me. He settled on it with me leaning back against his chest. Although he'd also built one for himself, my man didn't like us riding separately. If he had his way, we'd constantly travel on his krogi. But as he knew I was a speed junkie and absolutely loved the speeder he had made for me, he compromised by riding it with me. Technically, I should demand to be the one piloting my own bike, but I didn't mind feeling hugged by his strong and warm body while he chauffeured me around.

We took off at high speed, zipping past the poles that generated the protective energy field around the village. To think only a few months prior, they had prevented the Yurus from raiding and pillaging us when their previous Great Chieftain, Vyrax, had planned on turning every human into their slaves. What a long way we had come in such a short time, with Zatruk now leading his people on a much more peaceful and prosperous path.

As we raced deeper into the forest, I looked over my shoulder at Wonjin and kissed his jaw.

"You were fantastic tonight," I said in all sincerity. "You made me so very proud."

To my shock, the great tension I hadn't even realized had been stiffening his body bled out of Wonjin's shoulders. The look of both relief and vulnerability that flitted over his intimidating face messed with my head. He was so big, so strong, and so fierce when he brawled with his clanmates, I struggled to reconcile the fact that hidden beneath that fearsome exterior, the wounded child who got constantly bullied still lurked. For all his bluster, Wonjin had self-confidence issues.

"I'm glad you feel that way," he said, relief audible in his voice.

"I'm *always* proud of you, Wonjin," I said firmly and sincerely. "Our people have a rough past, and it will likely take a while for all the humans in Kastan to get over it. Don't forget that Luana was the first among us to marry a non-human native. But what anyone else thinks, including my parents, is irrelevant. All that matters is how *you* and *I* feel about each other. And I'm pretty damn crazy about you. What you said to my dad was accurate. You do make me feel cherished, protected, and respected. Don't ever think that you have to act in a certain way to avoid embarrassing me. I chose you for who you are. I'm proud of you just the way you are. And anyone who has an issue with that can take a hike. I'm keeping you."

My throat tightened at the way Wonjin scrunched his face. He was glaring at me, but I knew him enough now to recognize he was trying to hide the emotions surging through him. After all, he was a badass Yurus hunter. They didn't show soft emotions.

"I'm speeding through the forest as night is falling, woman. Now is not the time for you to shower me with sweet words," he grumbled in a chastising tone.

I laughed, kissed his jaw again and leaned back against him, facing ahead. My chest warmed with affection when he kissed the top of my head, and his arm around me tightened its hold.

Yeah, I was keeping my fluffy grump.

CHAPTER 6
WONJIN

We rolled up to the Kenthea Plateau where the arena and a large hotel for the guests would be built. My clan-mates had already started some of the excavation work. Dakas suggesting this location instead of the one we had originally planned on had been a great idea. The plateau offered a breath-taking view of the forest below and of the river beyond.

To my relief, we arrived with a few minutes to spare before the forest awakened. Lara had never witnessed the phenomenon up-close, only from above while flying her zeebis. The forests of Cibbos could be quite dangerous, especially back when we were the greater threat lurking by the human village.

There was so much more of our world's beauty that I intended to show her going forward.

We dismounted the speeder and walked hand in hand towards the edge of the plateau as the last lights of the sun faded on the horizon.

"Next time, I will take you directly to the heart of the forest so you can be surrounded by the plants and trees as they awak-en," I said in a hushed tone.

"I can't wait," she said with a grin. "I hear it's not just their looks that change but also their scent."

"Everything changes," I confirmed. "This is why carefully planning the tourist paths will be so important. Once the flora awakens, the landscape changes so much, they will get lost."

As if to confirm my words, a soft glow started appearing in the forest below, growing in intensity as it spread like a wave. Even the edges of the water lit up with the phytoplankton awakening. The trees shifted, reshaping themselves and exposing the colorful, glowing sides of their leaves. Plants and flowers folded in on themselves, revealing their inner sides which also bathed the forest with soft pastel lights.

"Oh, my God! This is breathtaking," Lara said.

"It is. Here is the place I believe we should set a hover lift to go down into the valley. And over there, is where we could create a path down for those who want to walk instead," I said, pointing them each in turn.

We spent the next twenty minutes discussing the matter, including the best location for a shuttle landing pad that could leverage the fantastic view. Zatruk wanted us to have a definitive plan by the end of the week. While we could have postponed this visit until tomorrow, Lara had insisted we do it tonight. Although she hadn't said it in so many words, my mate had wanted to give us an excuse to leave her parents' house if things hadn't gone well.

I still shuddered at the icy welcome they had given me. Frankly, I had expected them to kick me out before I could even sit at their table. But things had gone so much better than I ever could have hoped for. And above all, my female was pleased with me.

"I think we have everything we need," Lara said at last.

"Agreed," I said with reluctance.

She gave me an inquisitive look that had me shifting with embarrassment on my hooves. I wasn't ready for the evening to end.

Lara walked up to me and slipped her arms around my waist. I cupped her face between my hands and claimed her lips. As was her wont, she pressed herself against me, her hands gliding up my back. Her lips parted, welcoming my invading tongue as her nails gently raked the fur patch between my shoulder blades.

A familiar flame sparked low in my belly. I fisted her hair on her nape and tilted my head to the side to deepen the kiss. Her soft moan resonated straight in my loin. My hand caressed its way down the soft curve of her back to rest on her behind. After giving her left cheek a squeeze, I pressed her pelvis harder against mine. My woman grinding her front against my blossoming erection set my blood on fire.

I broke the kiss, intent on nipping at the sensitive spot in the crook of her neck, but Lara stopped me. To my dismay, despite the delicious scent of her arousal fanning the flame of my desire, my woman pushed me back, her eyes locked on my lips.

"We should head out," she whispered, her voice thick with lust.

Her words felt like an icy shower. Had I been too bold? Had I somehow offended her? Did she—?

"Yes, of course," I said, confused. "I will take you home."

"No. Not home," she whispered, stopping me from turning away. "Let's head back to *your* place."

"To my…?"

My brain froze. Eyes wide, I stared at her, wanting to make sure I wasn't misreading her intentions.

Eyes flicking between mine, Lara gave me a timid smile. She placed her hands on my waist and gently caressed the sides of my abdominals with her thumbs.

"Yes. Take me to your house."

"Are you sure, my Lara?" I whispered, lust, tenderness, and wonder all raging inside me.

Her smile broadened, becoming more confident. "Yes, I am. I'm keeping you, remember?"

"My beautiful mate," I breathed out before kissing her again.

Feeling dizzy and elated, I picked her up without breaking the kiss. I felt her gasp then chuckle against my lips as I carried her to the speeder. To my dismay, Lara sat facing me, her legs over my thighs on each side of me.

The whole way back, she kissed my neck and chest, her hands appearing to be everywhere at once on my body. My pleas —although threats would be more accurate—for her to stop went unheeded.

"If you make us crash, I will spank you, woman!" I ground through my teeth.

"Promises of a good time aren't going to make me stop," she deadpanned before biting my neck, while her hand slipped under my loincloth.

That, too, resonated straight in my groin. I growled menacingly at my female, who just giggled some more. The rest of the way home, she subjected me to the most exquisite torture. Between her kisses and nips, her hands roamed around my thigh and pelvic area, directly under my loincloth. She teased and taunted, caressed and clawed, coming ever so close to my aching shaft without ever touching it. A good thing too, or I might have crashed us into a tree.

By the time we crossed the city gates, I was ready to erupt. With the clan gathered in the square, music playing while the females danced, I thanked the Ancestors I hadn't come in through the main entrance. I didn't need people knowing my business, let alone having some idiot like Tarmek smelling my arousal and making some offensive comment that would require me cracking his skull. As much as I loved a good brawl, right now, I had a very different type of tumble in mind.

I headed straight for the side door of my forge, which connected directly to the house. As soon as I stopped the speeder in front of the door, Lara lost all of her boldness. To my relief, she didn't look like she had changed her mind, but the truth of the moment was sinking in. Although we'd claimed each other exactly twenty-six days ago, we still had not been intimate. Granted, we had indulged in some increasingly heavy petting, but we'd never crossed the next step.

Initially, I had resisted to prove to my female that I was serious about us and to give her a chance to stop seeing my much larger body as intimidating—if not scary. After, it had never quite felt like the right moment. In hindsight, I wondered if officially introducing me to her family had been her way of conveying to me that she was finally all in. While she had claimed me, I had known Lara still had reservations about us. Tonight, for the first time, I truly felt confident that my woman wanted me… wanted *us*.

Unless I make a mess of things tonight.

My stomach dropped at that prospect. All the ways in which things could go wrong flashed through my mind. I forced them out and deeply inhaled the tantalizing scent of Lara's arousal.

Lifting my mate up with one arm behind her thighs, I set the speeder to follow before opening the door to the forge. Lara held on to my right shoulder with one hand, the other caressing the two braids in my beard. Eyes locked with hers, I blindly parked her speeder inside the forge then headed for the door connecting to the main house.

My woman had entered my dwelling on a few occasions over the past few weeks, but we'd mostly kept to the dining room and living area. While I'd briefly shown her my bedroom the first time I gave her the tour, I quickly brought her back down to safer areas to avoid unnecessary temptation. Now, it was the living area that I hastened through on my way to the stairs to the upper floor where the four bedrooms of my home were located.

We didn't say a word, our eyes doing all the talking. Despite the slight trepidation that emanated from her, Lara seemed to vibrate with the same hungry anticipation I felt. I crossed the hallway to the end before opening my bedroom door. It faced the sliding glass doors on the opposite side of the room, which led to the master suite's private balcony. Ignoring the sitting area to the left, I turned right towards the massive bed, which occupied a little over half the side wall.

Letting Lara slide the length of my body, I set her back onto her feet.

"Now is your chance to run," I said, my voice gravelly with need.

My mate held my gaze unwaveringly. Reaching for the hem of the black and gray patterned, knee-length dress, she lifted it up. In one swift movement, she got rid of the garment before tossing it to the floor near the balcony's door. My breath caught in my throat at the sight of my woman's nearly naked body. She was wearing a sheer black bra that hid nothing of the taut little buds of her breasts, and matching, barely-there panties. The tiny triangle—merely holding onto Lara by a set of strings—gave me a mouth-watering view of her shaven sex.

A growling purr of approval and unsated hunger rose from my throat. I stalked forward, pulling Lara into my embrace as I reclaimed her mouth in a voracious kiss.

Ancestors, she tastes so sweet!

Despite the fire raging in my loins and my all-consuming urge to tear her underwear off, toss her on the bed, and ravage her, I forced myself to keep a slow pace. If I didn't handle our first night together properly, I could drive her away forever.

Still standing at the foot of the bed, we exchanged more kisses and caresses. I never thought the furless skin of a human could be so soft. I loved the feel of its silky texture against me. It erupted in a million little bumps, when I broke the kiss to trail my lips down the slender curve of her neck. I chuckled smugly as a shiver coursed through my female. She called this phenomenon goosebumps—a term that I found highly amusing —although in this instance frisson would be more accurate. While I had never seen a real-life goose, I could see the parallel with the bumps covering a plucked bird's skin. But ultimately, what mattered was that my touch had provoked a powerful enough emotional response to trigger this reaction.

As I brushed my lips down her clavicles to the inviting valley between her breasts, my fingers reached for the magnetic clasp of her bra, freeing my prize—the twins, as she liked to call them. They were a wonder to behold, round and perky, at least double the size of a Yurus female's breasts. Until my Lara, I'd never been particularly drawn to a female's breasts, but hers made my mouth water. It was that taut little button teasing me, and the brownish-pink circle of her areola that kept beckoning me.

I swiftly removed my woman's bra and greedily took one of her nipples in my mouth. As I licked and sucked on it, I reveled in the way it further hardened over my tongue. Lara sighed and slipped her fingers through my hair, pushing her chest forward for greater contact. With one hand, I fondled her other breast and occasionally pinched her little bud, not so much it hurt, but enough to give her a nice sting. With the other hand, I caressed the back of her leg, my palm eventually settling on the flimsy string of the nearly non-existent garment she called a thong.

My initial plan had been to take it off her, but I decided to turn my female around instead, reluctantly letting go of her nipple with one last bite. Standing behind Lara, I brushed her hair aside then I nipped at her nape before soothing it with a few kisses. As I trailed the length of her spine with my lips, I slipped a hand in front of her to caress her breasts some more. During our heavy petting sessions, I'd discovered how sensitive they were for my mate. So I wanted to give them all the attention they deserved.

Following a downward path, I kissed the small of her back then finally leaned away to get a full view of the wonder that was her behind. Ancestors! The plump and perfect roundness of each cheek was further enhanced by the string of her thong, which disappeared between the seam of her bum. Unable to resist, I leaned forward and gave her left cheek a proper bite. Lara gasped, yet arched her back, pushing her rear even more towards me.

Happy to oblige, I continued to kiss and bite her behind while lowering her thong. It slipped down her slender legs, and Lara stepped out of it. She'd no sooner put her foot back down than I pushed her forward. She raised her arms in front of her, catching herself at the edge of the bed. Her yelp of surprise turned into a strangled moan when I buried my face between her thighs to lick her slit. *Jaafan!* She was already soaking wet for me, her essence the most divine nectar on my tongue. She pushed onto her toes, lifting her rump to give me better access, while whispering my name in a needy voice.

Even with her moans confirming she was enjoying my ministrations, I felt cheated by my inability to fully feast on her, and especially on that sensitive little nub—from this position. Still pleasuring my woman with my mouth, I swiftly removed my loincloth, the only garment a Yurus male ever wore. That task done, and without warning, I pulled Lara back up and turned her around to face me. Before she even knew what was happening, my mouth was latching on to her clit. She cried out and slightly lifted her right leg, her hands holding on to my horns. As soon as she did that, something snapped inside me.

Slipping my arms behind her knees, I lifted her legs over my shoulders. She didn't resist, her grip tightening around my horns while she continued to moan. Without slowing my ministrations, I got back up on my hooves, my tongue alternating between dipping in and out of my female and teasing and licking her engorged little button. Lara ground her sex against my face, surrendering herself trustingly to me. Although she held onto my horns, and despite the fact that the mattress was just a couple of steps behind her to catch her fall should it occur, I held her back with one hand as I continued to feast on her.

Soon, my mate's legs began shaking around my face, her

breathing becoming shorter and louder as she began to crest. The sound of her impending release had my cock throbbing with need. Then she kicked her legs up with a sharp cry. The way she threw her head back as her climax swept her away, Lara would have fallen backward had I not held her.

I continued lapping at her while she flew high until the tremors shaking her body faded. Lifting her off my shoulders, I slowly kissed my way up her body as I lowered her in front of me without putting her back on her feet. Instead, I reclaimed her lips as I walked to the edge of the bed and sat down. I placed her in my lap, facing me.

With a lustful haze still lingering on her face, Lara slightly tensed upon feeling my stiff length between us. She pulled back, glanced down between us, then licked her lips nervously.

"Do not fear, my mate," I said, my voice thick with desire. "I will not hurt you. The night is young, and we have all the time in the world. We will go at your pace and do nothing more than what you are comfortable with. Do you understand?"

She smiled and nodded. "I do. I trust you. I want everything with you."

My heart swelled with the deepening affection I felt for this female… my woman. I captured her lips in a tender kiss. The searing flame that had been slightly cooling in response to her wariness, flared again when I felt Lara's hand close around my length. I gasped against her mouth, before breaking the kiss to look down.

She was timidly exploring my cock, her touch both curious and tentative as she traced the rippling ridges of the five rings at the base of my shaft. Lara paused at the second ring from the bottom, this one much wider and thicker than the others.

"That's my bulb," I whispered in response to her unspoken question. "Once you agree to become my wife, I will use it to knot with you when we couple. It will help increase the chance of us conceiving."

"To become your wife?" she exclaimed.

To my delight, she didn't look horrified, but displayed a mix of awe and surprise at my words.

I nodded. "Humans require a long period of courting before it is deemed appropriate to propose. So I am biding my time. But make no mistake, my Lara. You are mine. I *will* marry you. Until then, I will make sure you will never want another but me."

As I spoke those words, I slightly lifted Lara to push my cock below her, exposing my *vylus*. Lara inhaled sharply at the sight of the small appendage on my pelvis, just above my shaft. Shaped like a thumb with little bumps to provide extra sensations, my *vylus* would flick from side to side at the pace I voluntarily set to massage a female's sensitive spots. Yurus females didn't have a clitoris like human women. Instead, they had a *vyltia* made of half a dozen small, highly sensitive, nipple-shaped bumps above their slit. While our females rarely climaxed from penetration, a few flicks of our *vylus* against their *vyltia* would have them falling apart in no time.

And Lara's clitoris was about to get a similar treatment.

I pressed her pelvis against mine. The minute I activated my *vylus*, Lara emitted a throaty cry, and her nails on my shoulders dug into my flesh. I growled in approval, wishing she'd claw me harder. I accelerated the motion, one hand resting on her behind to keep her tightly against me. In seconds, my woman was nearing the edge again. Holding her nape, I slightly bent her backward—which only had her clit press even more against my *vylus*—and leaned forward to suck on her right nipple.

To my shock, Lara grabbed the single braid that held the upper half of my hair tied back and yanked it hard enough to make me raise my head away from her breast. Before I could understand what was happening, she claimed my mouth in a brutal kiss as she ground her sex against mine. There was something desperate and primal in the way our tongues warred and that she touched me. I was dying with the need to lift her up and impale her on my cock before losing myself in her.

When her second orgasm slammed into her, Lara shouted against my lips, her arms tightening around me with a strength I never expected from someone this fragile-looking. She buried her face in my neck while still grinding against me. My hands roamed all over her body as the heat of her feverish skin seeped into me.

Only once her trembling started receding did I finally lay her down on the bed. I stretched next to my woman, kissing her and caressing her, my hand venturing south. Eyes locked with my mate, I started inserting one finger inside her, then a second. Moving them in and out, I worked her until she loosened a little before inserting a third finger.

Despite the fire burning inside me, a sliver of fear poked its head again seeing how tight Lara was. Taking Zatruk and Rihanna as an example, I'd always felt confident that Lara and I would easily come together. Now, I wondered if I could truly fit without hurting her.

As if she had guessed what troubling thoughts were coursing through me, Lara suddenly pushed on my shoulder, forcing me onto my back. She climbed on top of me, rubbing her sex over mine, coating it with her slickness. My breath caught in my throat when she aligned the head with her opening.

It embarrassed me to admit I had asked Zatruk for advice on mating with a human. Having lost my father to Blood Rage as a child during the last Great War among the Yurus, I never had much of a father-figure. While I didn't consider Zatruk as a father—not with us being so close in age—he'd become a bit of a big brother since his wife had adopted me as a baby brother. Although it had been a slightly awkward conversation, he had suggested I let my woman set the pace and be the one to take as much of me as she could handle instead of me trying to push myself inside her.

That she had voluntarily taken that approach made me wonder if she had had a similar conversation with Rihanna. But all such thoughts quickly faded as I refocused on my mate and the feel of her around my cock. As expected, her body fiercely resisted my invasion. She'd barely gotten the head in while pushing herself down, retreating a little, then lowering herself some more.

My abdominal muscles contracted painfully with the need for me to thrust upward into Lara. Grinding my teeth to repress the urge, I slipped a hand between her thighs and gently massaged her clit as she continued her efforts to take me. Slowly, painstakingly, she took more and more of me, her inner walls squeezing my head in the most exquisite torture. Then, as she'd gotten me halfway in, her body suddenly yielded, and I found myself fully sheathed. We both cried out at the burning sensation.

Holding her close, I peppered kisses over her face and whispered words of love and encouragement while giving her body a chance to adjust to my girth. I couldn't say how long it took. The only thing that kept me from going into a sexual frenzy was the need to protect my mate.

And then her inner walls started contracting around my length.

I took that as the signal for me to start moving. With my hands cupping each round cheek of her behind, I slightly lifted her before carefully thrusting upward into her. That first stroke nearly had me coming undone. *Jaafan!* It felt so insanely good inside her. Lara's inner walls squeezed me from all sides, the searing heat of her sheath fueling the inferno raging in my loins.

When she pressed her hands to my chest, pushing herself up, I initially feared pain had prompted her to put some distance between us. To my relief, my woman started gyrating above me instead. Eyes closed, lips parted, her labored breathing mixing with her moans, my mate looked like a goddess.

Although I gradually picked up the pace, my teeth remained

clenched as I tried to keep myself from giving free rein to the insatiable hunger Lara stirred in me. I wanted to pound into her, wrap myself around every single centimeter of her naked body, feel her heat against me, drown in her delectable scent, and savor the salty taste of her skin. But this night was all about her pleasure.

However, Lara seemed to have a different idea in mind.

Instead of the slower and controlled rhythm I had set, she sped up her gyrations over me, spurring me on to go faster and take her harder.

I gladly complied.

Ancestors! I thought I'd die with bliss as I thrusted upward deeper into my woman. Liquid fire swirled in my nether region before shooting outward through my veins, setting each of my nerve endings ablaze. Her face strained by what looked like pleasure too much to bear, Lara was staring at me with hooded eyes, her nails digging into the fur patches on my chest. The slapping sound of our flesh meeting, my woman's throaty moans, and my nearly feral grunts permeated the room.

When she began to tremble above me, her labored breath coming out in faster, shorter bursts, I set my *vylus* in motion. It flicked from side to side at the highest speed I could achieve, massaging my mate's clit each time I thrust upward into her. Within seconds, she fell apart with a sharp, almost tortured cry before collapsing on top of me.

I closed my arms around her, holding her tightly against me, the searing heat of her skin against mine burning me like a thousand suns. While kissing her face and neck, I continued to pump in and out of her from below, my *vylus* working its magic on her little nub. My mate never got a chance to come down from her current orgasm before another crashed into her.

This time, her inner walls clamping down on my cock in an effort to force my own climax as she fell apart snapped something inside me.

With a savage roar, I flipped us around, and slammed myself home. Still half flying high and half-dazed, Lara barely gasped in response to my brutal invasion. She clung to me as I pounded into her with wild abandon, my moans sounding more like savage growls to my own ears.

Jaafan! I felt on the verge of combusting and my mind fracturing. This was too much, too intense. And yet, I wanted more. My female's hands all over my body, her breathy voice chanting my name and begging me not to stop sent me into a frenzy. My balls drew up and an almost painful heat flared in my loins as the need to climax rode me hard.

But I would only take that journey with my Lara.

With my *vylus* going into overdrive on her clit, I shifted my angle until my cock struck that legendary sensitive spot inside a human woman. In only a handful more thrusts, Lara's body seized. She shouted my name, her nails digging into the small of my back while her inner walls seemed to want to crush me.

This time, I joined my voice to hers and roared my release.

I slammed myself deep as ecstasy in its purest form shot out of me in waves. My head spun, and my skin tingled. I remained still for a few seconds to regain my bearings, then leaned down to reclaim my mate's lips while resuming thrusting in and out of her until the last of my seed was spent.

Feeling wrecked, I let myself drop to the side and rolled onto my back, drawing my female on top of me in the process. Boneless, Lara rested her head on my chest, a blissful expression on her face as she continued to shiver on top of me.

"You are mine, Lara," I said, my words slurred. "I'm never letting you go."

Although she didn't speak, her voice likely shattered from crying out so much, she tightened her embrace around me and kissed my chest.

I smiled.

EPILOGUE
LARA

The next few months went by like a dream. Wonjin was truly the perfect boyfriend. Nothing fazed him, and he was open to anything. Whether I wanted to go white water rafting, or cuddling on the couch watching some romantic movie, my man was down for it. At first, I worried that was a sign that he might be a pushover. Thankfully, I couldn't have been more wrong. Wonjin was no doormat. He had no qualms putting his hoof down when he disagreed with something. But his inquisitive mind always found something to learn about every experience.

Although he loved action and martial arts movies—especially the ones featuring some underdog wannabe fighter rising to fame—he always welcomed romantic movies. He called it research to better understand human courting rituals. When I argued that he had already caught the girl, he would counter that catching her was only the first step. Keeping her was the real challenge. And he firmly intended to do just that with me.

Did I melt and feel all kinds of warm fuzzies inside? Yep, I sure did.

That our movie nights usually ended in some wild and unbridled sex marathon certainly didn't hurt. Then again, any excuse justified us going at it like rabbits.

To think I'd been terrified of intimacy with him! Sure, he was quite literally hung like a bull, but he was always so attentive to me and my needs, I'd never felt safer. The chain orgasms were also a considerable bonus. Wonjin had my vagina singing arias all night long. I no longer cared if I walked crooked in the morning and that anyone noticed.

Granted, things had been a little awkward at first back in Kastan. We were a small colony of barely three thousand souls. Everyone knew everyone. Considering the previously violent interactions between our peoples, many humans continued to feel resentment and distrust towards the Yurus. While no one dared to make snide remarks to my face, I didn't miss the disapproving stares and the cooler treatment I received from some of them.

Saying it had not bothered me would have been a lie. However, if I looked at it objectively and not as the 'slighted' party, a part of me understood where they came from. Had I been in their shoes, living exclusively in Kastan without the constant interaction with the Yurus I enjoyed because of the project, I'd probably also give the side eye to anyone who started sleeping with the former enemy.

Thankfully, things steadily changed over the past couple of months, even though it would take much longer before full trust and acceptance would be achieved between our people. This was all due to more Yurus spending time in Kastan. As they would ensure security in the village once the guests and visitors arrived for the opening of the arena, the rest of the colony got to interact more frequently with them,

Even if they hadn't warmed up to the Yurus, that wouldn't have changed a damn thing. I was head over heels in love with my Wonjin. In fact, I hadn't slept in my house in Kastan in weeks. Half of my clothes had established permanent residence in Wonjin's closet—which he'd expanded to make room for me since Yurus really didn't have much of a wardrobe.

I'd unofficially moved in with him. Frankly, I'd been waiting for him to finally make it official, but he didn't seem particularly in a hurry to do so, which made me nervous. Mateo Torres—who was our colony leader and Luana's father—had made some less-than-subtle inquiries about me possibly putting my house up for vacation rental for dignitaries and wealthy visitors who came to attend the tournaments in the arena. It was spacious, elegant, and perfectly situated in the heart of Kastan, near all the amenities and social venues of the village.

I'd be more than willing to part with it and start my new life in Mutarak with Wonjin. If only the wretched male would make his move! I blamed all the romantic movies we'd watched together that always promoted a long dating period followed by an even longer engagement. Where the fuck was Kayog when you needed him to confirm you were the perfect match?

After one last critical look in the mirror, I gave my attire an approving nod. The long black pants hugged my waist and hips in the most flattering fashion. My sleeveless black top, with a plunging neckline gave a sexy glimpse of my breasts without going into slutty territory. A simple gold chain, gold earrings and a matching bracelet completed the outfit. My hair had been the biggest challenge. Wonjin loved running his fingers through it. Therefore, I'd debated long and hard between an updo or letting it loose. But as my top also had an enticingly revealing back, I settled on a messy bun.

I hurried to my parents' house located a block down from mine so that we could travel together to the arena for tonight's grand opening. Wonjin was already there putting the final touches with Zatruk and the rest of his clan.

The speed at which the door opened when I knocked betrayed the impatience and excitement my parents felt at finally witnessing the fruit of many months of intense collaborative work between the three dominant species inhabiting Cibbos. The future of this planet, and in particular of the Yurus, depended on the success of this event.

The warm smile on my face instantly faded at the sight of my father's unimpressed expression when he looked at me.

"What?" I asked, wondering how I had fallen short this time.

"Why are you all covered up with those long pants?" Dad asked in a disapproving tone. "It's not winter. You have pretty legs. Show them."

"Those pants are flattering to my figure!" I exclaimed, shocked my very conservative father would want me to show more skin. "Frankly, I expected you to complain that my top is too revealing!"

He scoffed and waved a dismissive hand. "You have a non-human boyfriend. See how he exposes his attributes to you by only wearing a loincloth? The females of his species also cover very little. How will you get him to marry you if you keep dressing like a cloistered nun?"

"What? I don't—"

"Your father is right," my mother said, interrupting me with a stern voice. "In Rome, do like the Romans. It's been many months. You all but live in his house, and he hasn't proposed. Let me fix that."

Stunned, I was too shocked to react when my mother grabbed my hand and all but dragged me to their room. Still speechless, I watched her rummage through her closet, before pulling out a black skirt.

"Mom, a change of clothes will not make Wonjin ask me to marry him! We've only been dating for six months. On Earth, humans date for years before making that kind of commitment!"

"We're not on Earth, and he's not human," she said in a tone that brooked no argument. "Put this on."

"But—"

"*Now*, Lara," Mom said, extending the skirt towards me with a 'You're not too old for me to spank you raw if you don't listen' look on her face.

I almost dared her to try to spank me, but the skirt was truly beautiful, and my mother's favorite. She'd never let me wear it before, even though I had asked in the past. It was an asymmetrical, layered, black chiffon skirt that would fit perfectly with my top. As my mother was shorter than me by a good head, the skirt would fall mid-thigh for me instead of being knee-length like it was for her.

I chewed my bottom lip, the opinionated and independent side of me wanting to refuse on principle, but the other side who always wanted to wear the skirt was screaming for me to accept.

"Lara?" Mother repeated sternly, waving the skirt in front of me.

"Fine, you bully!" I said, taking the skirt from her. "But only to keep the peace."

By the look Mom gave me, she wasn't buying my argument. Truth be told, I didn't care much. I slipped on the skirt and had to admit I looked sinfully hot wearing it.

"By the way, this skirt is called 'come back to Mama,'" Mom warned.

I gave her my most innocent look with a sickly-sweet smile. "Of course. You'll just have to remind me to bring it back if I forget."

My mother glared at me, likely kicking herself for lending me her favorite skirt.

"Now let's go. We don't want to be late."

I rolled my eyes at the approving glance my father gave me when we came out of the bedroom. Although I rejoiced that my parents had so thoroughly warmed up to Wonjin, it upset me that they were counting the days until we were officially married. I wished they wouldn't stress me out about it. While I genuinely believed Wonjin was in love with me, their comments fueled my insecurities. It wasn't like we'd been dating for years, and he was still giving me the run around. The past few months had also been extremely busy preparing the opening of the arena. So...

Heaving a sigh, I led my parents to the shuttle service we'd built in the village with direct flights to the arena and the main touristic venues and hubs we set up in preparation for the arrival of our guests and visitors. I had traveled in those shuttles multiple times over the past few months. But seeing them finally serving their purpose with real customers filled me with pride as I'd been part of the team designing them.

A mix of fear and excitement swirled through me as we entered the arena through the private entrance reserved for the staff and clan members. A human security guard—one of the many off-worlders who had accepted job offers on Cibbos in the hopes of a better life—ushered us to the VIP box, which over-looked the entire arena.

I walked in to find Rihanna, Graith—the leader of the Zelco-nians—his Lead Councilors Skieth and Dakas, Luana, Mateo, Counselor Allan, Jerdea, and Wonjin. My man immediately rose from his chair, a look of awe on his face as he took in my appear-ance. He swiftly came to welcome me at the door with a tender kiss, before paying his respects to my parents. Holding my hand, he led us to our seats. I stopped along the way to greet the others before settling down. Everyone shared the same air of wonder and excitement I felt.

A hush descended over the crowd as the opening ceremony began with highly choreographed dances and stunning visual effects, the haunting singing of the Zelconians, and breathtaking aerial displays and acrobatics involving the zeebises, their human riders, and the Zelconians.

After the last performance, the intergalactic gladiators paraded into the arena. I couldn't help but shake my head at how Wonjin perked up, the predatory glimmer in his dark eyes hinting at his eagerness to brawl with many of them. I silenced the worry that lingered at the back of my head that he could get seriously injured during the competitions. However, the security measures we'd instated helped alleviate most of them. Chief among them was the presence of Zelconians whose empathic abilities would warn them if any fighter intended to break the rules or use underhanded tactics that could result in grievous harm.

Once all the gladiators were inside the arena, we watched, mesmerized, as giant pieces of molded deutenium overhead spun and rotated, moving towards each other to form a massive mask of Mugrak, the Yurus God of War. Its eyes, made of red Zelconian crystals, lit up, sending a thrill down my spine.

My hand slipped into Wonjin while Zatruk addressed the crowd from the dais overlooking the arena. His welcome was short and to the point, his warnings stern, and his excitement palpable.

"The rules are few but will be strictly enforced. Break them, and we will gladly teach you the error of your ways. Fight fiercely and with the pride of your ancestors. Win with honor. Lose with grace. Stand toe-to-toe with the finest and make history," Zatruk said in closing.

The crowd erupted in cheers, while many of the gladiators filed out of the arena. Those remaining prepared for the first round which would start imminently. Moments later, Zatruk joined us in the VIP box. He made a beeline for his mate, picking her up like she weighed nothing—which was probably the case for a male of his tremendous strength—and crushed her lips in a passionate kiss.

My throat tightened with emotion at the striking tableau they formed. She was as tiny and dark-skinned as he was massive and pale due to his albinism. But everything about them and about that embrace screamed infinite love and utter triumph over adversity.

I glanced at Wonjin and was shocked to find him staring intensely at me, the oddest expression on his face.

"You know that I love you, right, my Lara?" Wonjin asked, his voice filled with tension.

"Yes, Wonjin. And I love you, too. With all my heart," I said, my pulse suddenly picking up.

He raised a massive hand, resting it on my cheek before gently caressing my lips with his thumb.

"You are everything I want, now and always," he whispered, his eyes flicking between mine.

"You're also everything I want," I echoed, my pulse cranking up another notch.

He smiled, his fearsome face melting into an air of pure love and adoration that turned me upside down.

To my surprise, he shot to his feet and grabbed my hand. Pulling me after him, he made a beeline for my parents, sitting on the raised row of seats behind us. One look at Wonjin's tense expression had my father getting up on his feet, quickly imitated by my mother.

"Wonjin?" my father asked questioningly.

His ears beginning to flick frantically had my mother clasping her hands nervously in front of her, her eyes wide, while my stomach was doing a series of backflips. I could barely hear my own troubled thoughts through the clamor of the gladiators clashing below and the thundering of my heart in my ears.

"Mr. Kimura," Wonjin said, his deep voice slightly shaky in a way I'd never heard before. "I have been dating your daughter for many months now."

"You have," my father replied, his body tense, despite his neutral voice and expression.

"I love her with everything that I am. It hasn't been much time by human customs, but my heart is certain she is the one. So, with your permission, I would like to ask for Lara's hand in marriage," Wonjin said, his ears flicking going into overdrive, so much so he smacked the left one in annoyance, not that it helped.

Without waiting for my father's response—not that it was *his* decision to make—I squealed and threw myself into Wonjin's arms. He instinctively embraced me. I beamed at him, tears of joy welling in my eyes.

"Of course he consents," I replied in my father's stead. "*I* consent."

Wonjin's face melted with love, a smile starting to form on his lips before he stiffened and cast a worried glance at my father. While Mom made no effort to hide her joy, Dad put on his best nonchalant air, as if such displays were beneath him. But I knew him well enough to know he was shouting with happiness deep inside.

"It appears that my daughter wants you," Father said matter-of-factly. "So yes, you have my blessing."

Wonjin muttered a thank you before lifting me up like Zatruk had done with Rihanna, and claiming my mouth in a passionate kiss while the other guests in the VIP box applauded and congratulated us.

When Wonjin ended the kiss, movement at the edge of my vision drew my attention. It was my mother with a smug look on her face.

"I told you the skirt would do the trick," she mouthed silently while pointing at it.

I burst out laughing before looking back at my mate and rubbing my nose against his.

"I love you," I whispered.

"I love you more," he replied before kissing me again.

THE END

LARA

WONJIN

KROGI

ZEEBIS

PRIME MATING AGENCY

I Married A Lizardman
I Married A Naga
I Married A Birdman
I Married A Minotaur
I Married Wonjin
I Married A Merman
I Married A Dragon
I Married A Beast
I Married Krogal
I Married A Dryad
I Married An Incubus
I Married A Mothman
I Married A Catman
I Married Amreth
I Married Kayog

THE MIST

The Mistwalker
The Nightmare

DARK TALES

Bluebeard's Curse
The Hunchback

THE SHADOW REALMS

Destined to the Wraith
Destined to the Reaper
Destined to the Lycan

VALOS OF SONHADRA

Unfrozen
Iced

EMPATHS OF LYRIA
An Alien For Christmas

OTHER
True As Steel
Alien Awakening
Heart of Stone
Oops! I Summoned a Liderc

ABOUT REGINE

USA Today bestselling author Regine Abel is a fantasy, paranormal and sci-fi junkie. Anything with a bit of magic, a touch of the unusual, and a lot of romance will have her jumping for joy. She loves creating hot alien warriors and no-nonsense, kick-ass heroines that evolve in fantastic new worlds while embarking on action-packed adventures filled with mystery and the twists you never saw coming.

Before devoting herself as a full-time writer, Regine had surrendered to her other passions: music and video games! After a decade working as a Sound Engineer in movie dubbing and live concerts, Regine became a professional Game Designer and Creative Director, a career that has led her from her home in Canada to the US and various countries in Europe and Asia.

Facebook

https://www.facebook.com/regine.abel.author/

Website

https://regineabel.com

Regine's Rebels Reader Group

https://www.facebook.com/groups/ReginesRebels/

Newsletter

http://smarturl.it/RA_Newsletter

Goodreads

http://smarturl.it/RA_Goodreads

Bookbub

https://www.bookbub.com/profile/regine-abel

Amazon

http://smarturl.it/AuthorAMS